SWEET VALENTINE

AUBREE PYNN

KALIAH JAMES

"*A*re you sure you don't need me?" my assistant asked through my AirPods for the tenth time. I was going to hang up on her if she kept this up. Alisha had been on my line for more than an hour going over my schedule after my hiatus from the spotlight came to an end. Going over my schedule was the last thing I wanted to do. In fact, the only thing I wanted to think about was skiing, drunk skiing, and indulging in whatever food the catering staff was whipping up over the next two and a half days. I would think about my hectic life, my meal plan, and my trainer's disapproving scowl when I returned to Los Angeles.

Alisha was on vacation and still felt the need to wait on me hand and foot. I loved her for all her hard work, but she deserved to relish in the time off. I wish she would just take it and stop fretting over whether I would make it a few days without her. I was going to be just fine, and I needed her to enjoy her husband.

Alisha traveled around the world with me for the better part of the year. We barely had time to take it all in. Undoubtedly, I knew her husband missed her being at home. That was something that gave pause when it came to her. I wasn't sure if I wanted to continue our business relationship because her marriage to Peter was more important. She insisted that she could both, she wanted to be everything to both Peter and me.

From what Alisha relayed to me on nights where insomnia kicked in, Peter was more supportive than most when it came to her career choice. Before Peter, Alisha went through a slew of men who didn't approve of my constant presence in her life. When she met Peter, I did everything but lock them in a room and force them to seal the deal. I knew from the first time he laid eyes on her that they were meant to me. He loved her, and it made my heart flutter every time he gazed at her tenderly. Peter was a catch, and I needed her to keep him, she was so deserving of him.

"Lisha," I groaned in annoyance. "I am a big girl. I can manage a couple of days without you. Not to mention, your husband is going to kill me if I make you work on Valentine's Day. I am safe in the mountains at the Canbury Hotel. I will be sipping spiked hot cocoa, skiing, and eating my heart out with a bunch of strangers."

"Okay," she blew in defeat after silence fell between us. "But please call me if you need anything."

"You've done enough. You've got me a driver, one of the best rooms at this hotel after they said they were booked, and the flight was wonderful. Now, I'm going to hang up. I don't want to hear from you until I get back to LA. I love you." Hanging up the phone before she could open her mouth to utter anything else. I let out a low snicker over how meticulous she was over the details of my extravagant lifestyle.

Alisha Manning was the best assistant a girl could ever ask for. She'd become more like family than my assistant over the last seven years. Alisha was there when I was a struggling actress, sleeping on her couch and living out of a duffle bag. She knew me better than I knew myself at times. How I lived my life without her before was incomprehensible. It became second nature to lean on her, she was ever-present as my rock. She was the only one who knew me before my stardom and wanted absolutely nothing from me but to make sure I was okay. So, when she asked for a vacation around Valentine's Day weekend, I didn't hesitate to give it to her with pay.

I also wanted to have some time away from the city and regroup before my hectic schedule began. I'd landed two movie roles and was sure that I wasn't going to stop moving until the end of next year. I needed to get away from everything. The mountains of Montana seemed like the best place to do it. It would keep my profile low. I didn't want to dodge paparazzi while I sat by the fire drinking my spiked cider or have them jump out at me while I skied down the slopes.

The Canbury Hotel was known for being tranquil. I needed that more than I had the words to explain. My body was exhausted. Physically, mentally, and spiritually. I needed a reset. Making it a point to take care of myself this year, this was my first step. I could've chosen anywhere to relax, but I needed somewhere where all of the activities could take my mind off of my most burdensome trouble.

Loneliness.

Loneliness crept its wretched self in my life and took over. It had a seat at the table, a spot in my bed, and took half of the closet for its baggage.

Sure, I had Alisha, but that was it. I didn't have a family that I was familiar with to lean on. Once my mother passed away, it was just me.

I loathed the holiday season from Thanksgiving to Valentine's Day. Despising being alone, I didn't want to think about going through another holiday season without someone of my own to hold me. I was pushing thirty, and it was becoming depressing to be alone year after year. The men in this industry were fickle. I wasn't in the business of being anyone's beard, co-star, free ride, or side chick. Average men were intimidated by my presence, or they were seeking a come up that I had no intention of providing. The thought of providing for a man who failed to provide for himself repulsed me. I couldn't catch a break in my personal life. The failure alone was horrifying enough for me to shut out the idea of letting someone in. The thought that I was going to be alone for the rest of my life or like my mother used to say, beyond my childbearing years, horrified me just as much. I didn't want to settle for just anything, but I also didn't want to be alone with three cats.

On the outside, I had everything that a girl could want. A flourishing career, more money than I knew what to do with, a wardrobe that most would kill for, fame, and a very active social life. But when I went home at the end of a long day on set, the house that I tried to make a home was cold, morbid, and secluded. I tried getting a dog and a couple of plants. However, I quickly learned that I wasn't cut out to be a fur mommy or a plant parent. I was far too busy to dedicate time to giving all my love and attention to an animal and watering a few plants. I failed at them both, miserably. So, that left me with just my work and my things.

Lots, and lots of meaningless things.

Leaning back into the back seat of the Chevy Tahoe, I let out a sigh, finally relaxing. Scrolling through my iTunes, I found the perfect playlist for the hour and a half drive. I'd made three for my flight from Los Angeles to Montana for this getaway. The scenery of the snow-capped mountains was breathtaking. My senses were heightened watching the view become larger as we traveled further up. Running my index finger over my Oldies but Goodies playlist, I took my bottom lip between my teeth. Hitting shuffle, I wiggled deeper into the seat and closed my eyes.

"Girls you'd better watch out, some guys are only about that thing, that thing, that thing," Lauryn Hill sang into my ears causing me to exhale.

This was one of my favorite songs of all time. So, what if

she had a knack of not showing up on time for anything, the woman was a legend and deserved to be treated as such. Lauryn Hill had gotten me through the hardest hurdles of my life. I tried to push those thoughts to the back of my mind so I wouldn't regret it and want that old thing back. Being married wasn't all it cracked up to be. Especially, when it was the wrong man. Daniel couldn't love me right even if I wrote a manual on how. He was the absolute worse. Refusing to give him much thought I shook the sight of him out of my head. This week was solely for me to relax not become extremely irritated by the idea of him.

Arriving at the hotel, I smiled at the fresh blanket of snow covering everything I could see. Stuffing my AirPods into the pocket of my coat, I grinned like a child at sight before me. I was in awe.

"Wow," I blew looking around.

By now the driver had gotten out of the truck to grab my bags. "No, no." I really didn't want anyone to respond to my celebrity for the duration of my stay. I wanted to enjoy myself and mind my own business. I prayed that no one noticed me with a bare face and natural hair, either.

"Ms. James," he smiled kindly down at me. He'd been so pleasant this entire ride here. He even had snacks and wine which I'm sure was Alisha's doing. Even when she wasn't here, she was here.

"I know, I know," I huffed. "But Alisha isn't here to know whether or not you took them inside. So, if you just let me take those and promise to pick me up for my trip back home, I won't tell her."

Continuing to smile at me he nodded and stepped back after handing my bags over to me. "Our secret. Enjoy your weekend."

"You too. Have a Happy Valentine's Day," I smiled picking up my luggage and heading inside.

Admiring the décor of the lobby, it sent a warm fuzzy

feeling through me, it felt like magic. The cedar wood was painted white and the metal beams suspended across from awning to awning were black with huge lantern chandeliers hanging between each. The large windows let in the bright light from outside and opened the area up, making it seem bigger than what it was. The furniture was white with blush and navy accent pillows and throw blankets. The tables between each furniture set had small floral arrangements, magazines, and crystal-clear fishbowls full of chocolate assortments.

Releasing a satisfying huff of air, I hiked my bags over my shoulder and pulled my suitcase over to the reception desk.

"Good afternoon," the receptionist greeted with a wide smile. Her smile was just as warm as this building. Her rosy cheeks almost made her eyes disappear behind them. "Welcome to the Canbury Hotel where the magic will change your life forever."

"Do they make you say that?" I questioned with a snort.

"They do, only because it's true. I've seen people like you trudge through the door lonely looking for a getaway and leave with love in their eyes. You'll see. Mrs. Manning already informed us of your arrival. Your room is on the third floor. There is a private lounge area up there for your personal use. Enjoy your stay," she smiled sliding my key over to me. "I'll have Miles carry your things up for you."

"Oh, no," I rejected as politely as I could shooing the bellhop away. "I got it."

Choosing to ignore her read of my life I returned a smile, retrieved my key, and headed towards the elevator with my things in tow. The elevator, placed in the middle of the building, was encased in glass and offered a 360-degree view of everything going on in the dining room, at the bar, and in the lounge area. Without a doubt, I was going to enjoy every minute of this stay.

Reaching the third floor, I took a glance at my key as I

stepped off the elevator. There were only two rooms on this floor. It made me wonder what unfortunate couple Alisha had them boot out. The floor was empty. She definitely had a hand in this.

Pulling my bags towards room 301, I inserted my key and turned the lock. Pushing the door open exposed the crisp white room decorated with a few vases of red roses. Alisha just couldn't relax if her life depended on it.

Letting the door close behind me, I packed my bags up in the corner of the room and peeled my layers off. The first thing I was going to do before partaking in my weekend plans was to get some well-deserved sleep.

Stripping down to my panties and bra, I shuffled over to the bed and pulled the covers back. Resting my head on the pillows the smell of vanilla and lavender filled my nose causing the corners of my mouth to curl into a small smile. That scent combination was my favorite. Letting this be another thing that I added to the list to thank Alisha for, I settled into a comfortable position before drifting off to sleep.

Waking up a few hours later I laid on my back and stared up at the white awnings resting on each side of the ceiling fan. The structure of the room was identical to the lobby. I had my own in-room sitting area and a window that stretched from corner to corner. It overlooked the lake and snow-capped trees. I admired the privacy and view alike.

Taking a quick shower and getting dressed in a pair of leggings, a blue and white flannel shirt, and a pair of metallic Uggs, I headed down to the bar.

Settling into the white bar stool, I ordered a Cupid Punch. The ingredients enticed me as I read over it on the drink menu. Tito's vodka, peach schnapps, a splash of tonic water, hand-made grenadine from pomegranates, and garnished with a blood orange slice. It was indeed as delicious as it looked on paper. So good that I waved the bartender over for another before completely consuming the current one I held to my lips.

"Be careful with this, Ms. James," he chuckled. "Cupid Punch isn't anything to be played with."

"Let me take a wild guess, it'll have me falling in love," I mocked rolling my eyes glancing over the dinner menu.

"It will," he shared. "What are you having this evening?"

"I think I'll do the seared filet mignon with the roasted potatoes and sautéed broccolini," I shared looking up from the menu.

"Dessert or you'll hold off for now?"

I heard what he said, but my eyes were stuck on the man who appeared at the receptionist's desk. He had a scowl of aggravation etched across his caramel face. His jawline was tight and defined. Even under the coat, I could tell he was built. I didn't know what was happening to my mind but all the sense I possessed fled. Biting down on my lip I couldn't take my eyes off of him. I never saw anyone like him before. Had I worn panties under my leggings I would've gladly taken them off and handed them over to him. No questions asked and no strings attached.

"Him with strawberries," I let out a heavy moan the escaped from my depths. The sound of my lust to my ears snapped me out of my trance. If my chocolate cheeks could've beamed red, they would've.

"Excuse me?" the bartender asked raising his brow unsure how to respond.

"I'm sorry. I'll have the triple chocolate mousse cake with the strawberries on the side," smiling shyly at him. He nodded and walked down to the other end to make my drink allowing me to look back at the pensive stranger at the desk.

2

ANTONIO CLARK

*T*oday was in no way my day. This was not how I planned to spend Valentine's Day. I was flying from Philly to Portland when my jet made an emergency stop. I couldn't tell you where the hell I was. All I know is that after two cab rides and a bribe to the girl at the front desk, I was finally out of the snow and in a room. I should've been in Portland with Jada.

Jada.

Jada and I had been dating for a little over two years now. The last six months had been on and off between us, especially after I was traded to Philly from Miami. She refused to leave Miami to be in Philly with me. I could understand that the change in weather was something she didn't want. However, fact that she left Miami about two months ago to move back to Portland with her parents sent me through the roof. I'd never been the man to lie, cheat or take her for granted so I couldn't understand why she'd made that move so abruptly.

Not only did she pack up the house in Miami and move back to Portland a couple of months ago, but she also informed me during our last phone call that she'd mailed my things to Philly. And the kicker? We were over. As much as I didn't want to swallow the fact that this relationship was coming to an end, I felt it. The minute she threw a fit about coming to Philly, I knew it was only a matter of time. I was never going to be the man that stepped out on our relationship because I was lonely as hell up there without her. Instead, I patiently waited for her to acknowledge that she wasn't happy anymore and was ready to leave.

The part that pissed me off was hearing that she hadn't been happy well before the trade while I was in mid-flight to surprise her. I was told that I wasn't aggressive enough. I didn't get mad when she pushed my buttons. Apparently, what she wanted was a nigga to rough her up and push her around. That wasn't me. I was raised to have the utmost respect for women and to cherish the people I loved. Not only that, I was as laid back as they came. It took a lot to rile me up.

So, here I was in the middle of nowhere while I waited to hear the status of my jet. Since Portland and Jada were now out of the picture, I was going to inform the pilot that we were going to fly to South Carolina to see my folks. We played on Christmas Day, so I missed my family holiday. The more time passed without going home, the more I missed them.

Kicking off my Timberland boots and pulling my sweater over my head, I heard my stomach rumble reminding me that I hadn't eaten since being bombarded with an avalanche of shit. Dragging my tired body to the bathroom, I turned on the shower letting the steam fill up the bathroom. This was something I made a habit of since leaving my parents' house and paying my *own* water bill. It relaxed me. With everything going on I needed to be relaxed a little.

This place had no TV's, I barely had cell service, and there was absolutely no internet. I was in a white snow-capped hell and was counting down the days to get back to civilization. Even if civilization was considered to be the sticks of Lexington, South Carolina.

After showering, I threw on my Nike jogging suit and rode the elevator downstairs to the bar. Tonight, was the couple's trivia so the entertainment room was full of couples in bliss and the bar was empty. Well, almost empty. At the end facing the entrance was a woman I swore I'd seen before, but I couldn't put my finger on where I knew her from. She was thoroughly enjoying her dinner. Climbing on the barstool, I grabbed the menu and studied it before the bartender came around the corner with a rack of glasses.

"Hey man!" he greeted as I threw my head in his direction. "What are you drinking?"

"Jack and Coke," I answered placing the menu down and glancing across the bar again.

"Got it coming right up. What brings you to the Canbury Hotel on Valentine's Day weekend, alone? That's some serious torture," he chuckled making my drink.

"My jet blew an engine, so this was the only hotel within miles of where we landed. So, here I am. What's the deal with no TVs and Wi-Fi? Y'all are going to kill a brother," I grunted.

"Well, the Canbury is somewhere couples come to reintroduce their relationship to the magic again. Seems like you could use some yourself," he mentioned.

He was older and reminded me of my pops with his grey goatee, bald head, and dark skin. Instantly, I wondered where the hell he came from. Apart from myself and the woman across the bar, I hadn't seen any black people.

Scoffing at his remark of falling in love, I shook my head. "I'm good. Just ended a two-year relationship. Definitely not diving into another one anytime soon."

Whistling he shook his head. "Looks like you're in the right place, Mr. Clark. What are you eating?"

"How's that filet?" I asked. Being in the middle of the

11

mountains I didn't dare to ask about the seafood. I didn't trust it. After living on the east coast my entire life, all my seafood had to be fresh and never frozen.

"Oh, it's good," he nodded. "It comes highly recommended."

"Let's do that with the mashed potatoes and roasted veggies. Another one of these won't hurt either," I mentioned as he slid my drink over.

Nodding, he made another drink before heading off into the kitchen. Allowing me some time to myself.

Peeking across the bar again at the woman, I became lost for a second. I could've sworn she had some voodoo that took my lungs and squeezed them as tight as she could without lifting a finger. She was gorgeous. She wore no makeup, but her skin was flawless, and her eyes were wide. Her golden-brown skin danced under the low lights of the bar. Hands down, she was probably the most beautiful woman I'd laid my eyes on. I'd put my eyes on tens of thousands of women, but she took the cake.

Jada was pretty, but unfortunately, she couldn't hold a match to what I was looking at. Catching my eye, she squinted her hazel eyes at me before cutting into her steak and resuming her private session. Pulling my eyes away from her I brought my drink to my lips. Letting the alcohol take its course through my body I leaned back on the stool and pulled out my cell phone. Hoping for a little service, I groaned at an x where my service bars would typically be.

A few moments passed before I was enjoying my dinner. I could understand how the beautiful stranger across the way got caught up with her dinner. I hadn't had food like this since I left Florida.

My life in Philly was isolated, to say the least. It consisted of practice, games, take out, and home. I kept my head down and minded my business. It kept me out of unnecessary trouble. After Miami, I was good on my name not being mentioned for anything but my God-given talent.

Besides my teammates, I really didn't interact with anyone. I'd been that way since, Eddie, my brother, died. I could never forget that night no matter how hard I tried. I could still feel his hot blood splatter across my face. He was days away from going to college, and he got into an argument with a man over a gas pump. After the two walked away from each other, I thought that it was over. I remember Eddie settling into the driver's seat when the man strolled up to the car and shot my brother in the side of his face. Remembering how helpless, angry, and heartbroken, I felt while my brother's warm blood and brain matter covered my face.

Half of Eddie's face was blown off due to the gunshot forcing us to have a closed casket service. I think a piece of my heart was buried with him that day. I never imagined having to live my life without him. Since I was old enough to walk and talk it was the two of us joined at the hip. If it hadn't been for him pushing me into perfecting football, I would've never come this far. I owed him every success. Every win was for him and every loss I thought about what he would say I needed to improve. Even though he wasn't with me physically, his spirit always lingered around.

About three drinks later and a full belly it was time to sleep my troubles away. Tipping the bartender, I stood to my feet and headed off towards the elevator. Sticking my arm between the sliding door for it to open back up I stepped on and hit the button for the third floor before the doors started to close.

"Hold it," I heard a tiny voice approach the elevator. "Hold it!"

The Jack Daniels in my system slowed down my response time. Hitting the button for the doors to open, I saw the woman from the bar. Her hazel eyes were peering at me with irritation while she rubbed her shoulder.

"You didn't hear me?" she questioned with a groan of pain. She'd tried to ram her shoulder between the doors to make them bounce open.

Moving my head back and forth I wasn't in the mood to deal with anyone's attitude tonight. All I wanted to do was take my ass to my room and sleep. "Look, you're on the elevator, now. Just enjoy the ride."

Usually, I wasn't snappy but the time change, all the shit I went through today, along with the thought of Eddie sent me to the edge.

"Well, excuse the hell out of me," she blew standing off in the corner. She was clearly just as buzzed as I was, and I could see her battle with herself. She wanted to say more, but she pressed her lips together, folded her arms across her chest, and let out a deep exhale.

Good, I didn't want to hear anything.

Reaching the third floor, she whisked past me and off the elevator to the only door at the end of the hall. I couldn't believe that someone as beautiful as she came here alone. Drawing my eyes away from her plump ass, I stalked to my end of the hall. Unlocking my door and shuffling inside I let the door close behind me.

Removing my body out of my jogging suit I tossed it over the chair and fell into the pillows. Although there wasn't any service here, the view was spectacular and the moon shined brightly through the large windows across the room. Pulling the cover over my head, I yawned and drifted off to sleep.

The morning sun peeked its way over the mountain tops and trees in the distance, illuminating the room. The rays graced my bare chest as I stretched. I hadn't slept that good in weeks. My internal alarm clock was set for post-season training. My time was scheduled and today wasn't any different. I remember the receptionist mentioning that there was a gym located on the first floor. It was too early for me to eat breakfast, maybe a couple of miles on the treadmill would work up an appetite.

Covering my ears with my gold-wrapped Beats headphones, I started up the treadmill and began to run to Meek Mill's Championships. This album was now one of my favorites and got me through the monotony of running on a treadmill, like a hamster without the wheel. After six miles and a good stretch, I headed back to my room. Exiting the elevator, I looked down the hall. I wasn't exactly proud of taking my frustrations out on a total stranger the night before. It was only fitting to apologize for my actions.

I usually wasn't a man to put myself out there, but something about her drew me in. Also, we didn't exactly have a pleasant exchange yet. Hoping to turn that around, I tapped my knuckles against her door. Regretfully waiting on her to open the door, I tried to tell my feet to back up. They didn't. They were planted.

Seeing the door pull open she poked her head out and traced her eyes over me. With a squint of those eyes, she looked up at me oddly. "Okay…"

"So, I want to know if you'll join me for breakfast. Just as an apology for last night," I spoke up after clearing my throat.

"I don't know you," her eyes continued to squint with uncertainty.

"This is true," I chuckled nervously. "But if you meet me downstairs for breakfast you could. If you're downstairs in 15, I'll take it as a yes, if not no harm no foul."

Nodding her head slowly she flashed an uneasy smile before pushing the door closed.

I didn't know what my brain was doing, but I prayed I didn't regret mixing myself up with this girl. As beautiful as she may be, I didn't need another headache.

Kaliah James

THE SIGHT OF HIM MADE SOMETHING HAPPEN TO MY BODY. THERE was a wave of heat that came over me. Since the moment I laid eyes on him at the reception desk last night I knew that he was going to be the cause of a lot of trouble. I didn't come here to get fucked by some random stranger and put away wet. But I had a feeling that's exactly where this was going. For the life of me, I couldn't say that I didn't want it. The heat rising through my body confirmed it. He was standing at my door soaked in sweat caused the hairs on the back of my neck to rise on its ends.

I wasn't going to jump at the invitation in his presence. But I knew as I nodded my head slowly and closed the door that I was going to beat him downstairs. Not only was I hungry but I had an avid need to know who he was and why he had this magnetic pull on me. Honestly, it was nerve-racking the way my body felt. Even when we connected eyes last night, it took everything in me not be a hoe and invite him back to my room. Luckily, I was a trained actress, and I knew how to pretend well.

Wiggling my body into my black waterproof leggings and zipping my black quilted jacket up, I checked my reflection in the mirror. Tucking my hair behind my ears, I grabbed my beanie with the giant puffball on top and shoved it into my jacket along with my gloves. After sliding my feet into my black Uggs, I headed downstairs for breakfast. The plan for today was to hit the slopes. That would be just what I needed to cool myself down. I never met a man in all my days that pulled this unorthodox temptation from my being, and I didn't even know his name.

Making my way into the dining room, I smirked seeing that he beat me down here. He was sitting off in the corner peering out the window in deep thought. The light reflecting off of the snow into the window made him look heavenly. His smooth caramel skin glistened with some sort of mysterious power. Snapping myself out of my thoughts I approached the table as coolly as possible.

"Mind if I take this seat?" I asked standing behind the empty chair.

Standing to his feet, he smiled. The dimples in both cheeks were piercing, and his teeth were immaculate. I was a sucker for an excellent set of teeth. He had to be at least six foot five inches and about two hundred and fifty pounds of muscle. He wore a long-sleeve Dri-FIT Nike tee paired with Nike Dri-FIT pants. His bulging muscles were distracting me. The only thing I could think about was digging my pink manicured nails into them. I wished I had cell phone service so Alisha could talk me out of being the slutty version of myself.

Walking around the table, he pulled my chair out allowing me to take a seat before pushing it closer to the table. Settling back into his seat, he locked eyes with me. Pulling my eyes away from him was becoming a task.

"I guess a formal introduction is due," he continued to smile at me while his southern draw hypnotized me. Thank God I was sitting down because I was sure my knees would've buckled if I were standing. "I'm Antonio Clark, my friends and family call my Anton."

Stretching his large hand across the table, I lifted mine to connect with his. His hand engulfed mine. "Kaliah James."

"It's nice to meet you," he held my hand in his a few seconds longer before he released it from his custody. "Hungry?"

"I can always eat. That's without question," I smirked looking down at the menu.

"Hm," he grunted glaring at me with what I liked to call the light skin squint. "Not too many women I know who like to eat. It's always about what French toast can do to their hips."

Shaking my head, I smiled involuntarily. "Those women

were lying to you. We all like to eat. You know how they say the key to a man's heart is through his stomach…"

"And the way to a woman's heart is through the man's wallet?" he questioned causing me to chuckle and roll my eyes. "No?"

"Seems to me that you've been misinformed," I pointed out connecting eyes with him again. His eyes danced due to the light shining through the window. They were beautiful, they sat under his bushy brows, but they were intense and ebony in color.

"I see that," he smiled licking his lips. Breaking our eye contact, I looked back at the menu before the waiter approached us.

Greeting me with a long stem red rose. "Good morning, I'm Jacob, and I'll be your waiter this morning. Have you made your minds up?" he asked looking down at the two of us.

I really appreciated the staff's discretion about who I was. I felt normal for once. "I'll have the French toast with pouched eggs and the bacon on the side. Water is fine."

Ordering my food, I placed the menu down while Antonio pinned his brows together and put a finger on his chin. "I'll take the steak and eggs with the home fries. I'm good with water. Thank you."

Taking up our menus he walked away from the table leaving us alone again. "I got to ask…"

Giving him my attention, I traced his face with my eyes. "Shoot."

"Why are you here alone? On Valentine's Day weekend at that," he inquired.

"Well," I sighed. "I worked so much this year I was on the edge of being burned out, and I wanted to get away from everything. This place popped up on my google search, so I jumped at it. It's beautiful, and the couples in love don't bother me. It's refreshing actually."

"It doesn't?" he questioned raising his brow. "You really are different."

"I can only be what I can be."

3

ANTONIO CLARK

I was enjoying her company immensely. I didn't want to part ways. I felt myself loosen up for the first time in a long time. I was smiling and laughing, and it felt better than any accomplishment I'd ever made. It was mind-boggling how someone I just met could blanket me with this type of peace.

Breakfast was pleasant. We connected over our love for food, our peace, and our southern upbringing. I didn't ask her what she did for a living because I didn't want her to ask me. I liked being Antonio Clark the regular guy, not Antonio Clark, the superstar athlete. I couldn't draw back from her; she was captivating. "Have you ever skied?" she asked breaking our staring contest.

"You're kidding, right?" I released nervously. There was a lot I could do, but skiing wasn't one of them. Not wanting to say no because leaving her presence wasn't what I was ready to do quite yet, but I knew I was going to end up embarrassing myself.

"No," she smiled. "I'm not. Can you ski?"

"I can do anything," I boasted proudly sticking my chest out. Her laugh was infectious, and it made me smile.

"Don't agree on my behalf," she hummed pulling her gloves and beanie out of her jacket pocket. "I don't want you to embarrass yourself."

"Let's go," I chimed springing up from my seat. Trailing her to the door, I reached over her five-foot-five-inch frame holding the door leading to the outside open for her. Allowing her to walk through and across the freshly salted cedar porch, I relished at the sight of her hips swinging back and forth gracefully.

Surveying the area, I spotted couples sliding down the snowy hills on boards and donuts. The ski lift was a few feet away, and it rode through the trees. Wincing at the thought of falling on my ass I quickly sucked it up and followed her through the snow.

I felt crazy.

Here I was following a woman I hadn't known more than a minute and who hadn't even given me anything yet was able to make me putty in her hands. All I knew about her was the things that she shared. I didn't know what made her tick, or how she reacted when something irritated her. What I did know is that for the next day and a half I wanted to spend every waking moment with her.

Arriving at the ski check-in, Kaliah suggested the gear I should get especially with this being my first time. As an athlete, it was embedded into my DNA that I could do any and everything I put my mind to. This was no different.

"You got it?" she giggled helping me to my feet. Keeping her tiny hands on my core to steady me, I felt something strange. "It's like rollerblading, just glide through it."

"How the hell did you learn how to do this? Black people don't ski," I huffed, balancing myself.

"We can do whatever we want to do," she said in a matter of fact tone. "I won't let you go."

Helping me to the beginner's hill, we stopped at the top, and she let me go. I wasn't going to dare try anything steeper than this. I'd already put my pride on the line by making it this far.

"Alright so, you're just going to push off and glide," she demonstrated gliding down the slope with such ease. "You can do it."

She encouraged from the bottom with a smile just a bright as the snow.

"Anton, what the hell are you doing man?" I grunted to myself before mustering up enough nerve to push off, stumble, and roll down the hill. I could hear her yelps over my snow muffled grunts.

"Oh my God!" she shouted covering her mouth and rushing over to me as I was spread-eagled in the snow. "Are you okay?"

I could hear her laughter muffle behind her gloves. "Not funny."

"Actually," she smiled. If her chocolate skin could beam red, it would've. "It's was quite entertaining."

Stradling over me she outstretched her hands to assist me to my feet. With an uncontrollable giggle, she reached up and wiped the snow from my goggles. "You can quit now if you want."

"No," I chuckled. "I just know that skiing wasn't made for me."

"Maybe a ride on the lift?" she offered another activity. She didn't want to break away just as much as I didn't.

"I'll do anything that doesn't involve me tumbling into a pile of snow again."

With that, we returned our gear and found ourselves riding above the trees. The icicles hung from the branches, and the rays of sunshine reflected off of them. Kaliah didn't say much, she just enjoyed the view as much as I did.

Once the ride came to an end, she stopped in her tracks back to the hotel and smiled. "Thank you."

"No," I shook my head. "Thank you. I don't think I could have that much fun doing something I suck at."

"I'm sure you'll get the hang of it. Thanks for the apology," she chuckled with a glimpse of sadness in her eyes. I was sure I knew what that was about.

"Kaliah," I called as she started up the steps. Stopping her pursuit to look over her shoulder at me. "Lunch?"

Kaliah James

HOW COULD I SAY NO TO LUNCH? ALL THIS ACTIVITY DEFINITELY worked up my appetite. Not to mention the thought of breaking away from him made me a little sad. He was so much more than his fantastic physique, and I wanted to know more. When I was around Antonio all of my senses heightened. It was foreign. I'd never met a man who could do this to me. Not even my ex-husband enticed this sort of feeling out of me. It was addictive, and I wanted more and more of it. Thinking about the reality of it all put me at a pause. In a day and a half, we would be back to our separate lives while holding each other close as a memory.

Lunch was just as fabulous as breakfast. The main reason I booked my stay at the Canbury was solely because of their chef was world-renowned. I could live with being cut off from the outside world as long as there was good food.

"Tell me about you," he crooned in my ear while I tucked my legs under my butt. We'd gone from the dining room to the private lounge on the third floor. The fire was dancing, and the spiked cocoa in my mug was relaxing me more than my comfort level would allow.

"What do you want to know?" I asked looking into his eyes. I could stare into those eyes forever.

"Where are you from?" beginning his series of questioning.

"Alabama," I shared as he nodded. My accent hadn't left me after spending years in Los Angeles.

"Why are you here alone?" he pressed again. He asked this question earlier in the day. I thought my answer sufficed, but I see it didn't.

"Why are you here alone?" I returned the question with a question as I watched him sink deeper into the cushions of the chair and exhale. Rubbing his palm across his low haircut, he glanced at the fire.

"I was actually on my way to Portland. Where my girl-ex girlfriend recently relocated. Mid-air an engine blew on the jet, she broke up with me, and I landed here," he shared.

"How long have you two been together?" I asked. I wanted to draw away from him after learning about his baggage. How selfish would that be, I had my own. There's no way I could judge another soul about theirs.

"Two years but with the long-distance things haven't been the same. She wanted something and someone different. I can only be who I can be, so I let her go. I've never been the type of man to make anyone stay who didn't want to," he rumbled dragging his eyes from the fire to me. "Your turn. And when I ask why are you alone, I mean where is your man and is he going to pop out somewhere? I don't want no problems."

Laughing as he threw his hands up in defense, I shook my head. I hadn't laughed this much in a long time. Especially not with anyone of the opposite sex. With everything in Hollywood going array, I had to make sure I didn't seem too friendly or eager when I interacted with men. I didn't want the wrong message conveyed to anyone about anything.

"Well, I am single as a dollar bill," I shared. "Work keeps me going, so there isn't that much room to establish a solid love life."

"Wow," he let the air escape his lungs. Pinning my brow together I tilted my head to the side and looked at him.

"Wow?"

"No one is taking care of you," Antonio finally spoke up.

Sighing and squirming in my seat, there it went again. That irksome need to take all of Antonio in without hesitation.

"Hmm," I buzzed after gathering myself. I placed my mug down on the table and nestled into the cushions. "I would love that…"

"But…"

"But I don't want just anyone. I had just anyone, and it failed, and it broke my heart that I failed. Unlike you, I wasn't strong enough then to let it go. I held on until it almost sucked the life from my being. I was standing on the brink of losing it all. I had to make a decision. It was either going to be him or me. For the first time in my life, I chose me. I want an earth-shaking love, mountain-moving, faithful, and always enough. I don't need anyone to take care of me just because. I want a man who loves me and respects me enough to cherish every part of who I am," I shared.

Talking about my ex usually didn't happen. He didn't deserve any more life given to him. Raking my hands through my hair, I could feel Antonio's strong hands wrap around my waist causing me to hold my breath. I didn't know what was coming next, but I was welcoming it. If he knew that I'd thrown my inhibitions to the wind the night I saw him we would be doing more than talking about our past rela- tionships.

Wrapping my body up in his arms, he held me against his chest, and I melted like butter on toast. Flipping through the archives of my memory to remember the last time someone held me with such security. Concluding that it was so long ago, I let it go and lived at this moment.

What meant so much more to me than sex, was intimacy.

Soon, Antonio would be gone so I would have to savor every moment.

Realizing I'd drifted off to sleep in his arms, I lifted my head off of his chest. Antonio was sound asleep. Letting a smile part my lips I placed a gracious kiss on his jawline before easing off the couch. Taking the throw and draping it over his relaxed body I turned to head to my room.

4

ANTONIO CLARK

.

*W*iping my face, I grunted and looked around the private lounge area. I silently thanked God that this area was secluded to the third floor only and no one caught me with my mouth open. Sitting up, I stretched, seeing the half-drunken mugs of hot cocoa, the dying fire, and the empty spot that Kaliah took up the night before. The need to be closer to her was becoming irrefutable. Every time I told myself to pull away from her, I ended up closer to her. I needed her close to me for as long as I could have her.

Laying the blanket over the arm of the couch I dragged my body into my room and set my alarm for 10 am. That gave me five hours to sleep before I was knocking on Kaliah's door again like a crack head feening for another hit of whatever she'd given me. Since meeting Kaliah, Jada had been the furthest thing from my mind. Even when I was talking about her last night, I felt nothing. The need to give it any more thought was over, I'd been exposed to something new.

Waking up and getting ready for my day I observed myself in the mirror. I had no plans of being in the snow today, so I got dressed in a sweater and jeans. It was Valentine's Day. This was the first year I'd been without anyone to shower with gifts. You could say I was a bit of a Casanova when it came down to it. I got it from my pops. I longed to have what he built with my mom. Their love was something to rival anyone's relationship goals.

Kaliah didn't strike me as the type of woman who needed to be flooded with gifts. If I were with her beyond this weekend, I imagined that she was just as laid back as I was. Once she was home from a long day, she didn't want any distraction from the outside world.

Thinking about her beyond tomorrow was going to be torture for me. The way her body melted against mine as if it belonged there solidified that notion. Grabbing my room key off the dresser, I walked out of the room and down the hall.

Upon reaching her door, I could hear music playing from behind the door.

I wasn't looking for this
What is this?
I don't know
You know I was doing just fine
By myself
On my own
Tell me how to stop this feeling

It was sultry and conveyed everything I felt. Kaliah was fucking my mind up. Everything I thought I knew flew out the window the minute I made contact with her. Maybe the myth of the Canbury Hotel was true.

I don't want to fall in love
Just want to have a little fun
Then you came and swept me up
And now I'm done so done

I tapped my knuckles against the door hard enough for her to hear it over the music then stepped back and leaned on the wall adjacent to the entrance of her room. My heart thundered in its cage, and my palms were sweaty. This woman was breaking me down. I had the right mind to run. Hearing the door open I cut my eyes in the direction to see her poke her head out and smile like she knew what I was going to say.

"You left me hanging last night. Snoring with my mouth open and drool running down my face," I playfully shook my head squinting my eyes at her. She giggled, covering her mouth. I couldn't help but smile. "I think you owe me an apology."

"I'm sorry," she continued to giggle.

"That's not the apology I want," I licked my lips looking down at her. What I wanted was her spread open across my bed cursing my name, but I wouldn't dare be that forward with a woman of her caliber.

"What do you want?" she asked with her interest piquing and a light bite to her juicy bottom lip. I got the vibe. It made my dick jump slightly in my pants. Watching her bite down on her supple bottom lip made me want to take it between my teeth and do the work for her.

"Get dressed, breakfast is almost over," leaving my orders at her threshold I turned to walk away. I was seconds away from entering her room and expressing to her how she'd made me feel.

I opted to take the stairs so I could jog some of this energy off. The staff was busy preparing for the Valentine's Day ball this evening. Purchasing some roses from the front desk and a token of appreciation for her time, I finalized my transaction and entered the dining room. Scanning the area, I located our table off in the corner. About five minutes passed until she joined me. Wearing a pair of dark distressed denim jeans and a yellow crop top sweater I revered the view as she strolled towards me like she had no care in the world.

Standing to my feet as she approached me, I greeted her with a hug and kiss on the forehead. "Happy Valentine's Day."

Kaliah's smile crossed her face like lighting. She smiled so wide her eyes disappeared behind her cheeks. "You didn't have to. Thank you, Anton."

My dick jumped again.

Anton.

This was going to become annoying if I didn't do something about it, soon.

"It's the least I could do," I rumbled in her ear, inhaling her scent. Her skin oozed hints of vanilla and lavender. Whatever it was that she wore was going to make a nigga come out of character, recklessly.

Pulling her seat out for her to sit down, I pushed her closer to the table before taking my place across the table. Watching as she admired the bouquet of roses, I smirked in satisfaction.

"What are you doing tonight?" I asked smoothly looking at her from under my bushy brows.

"What is there to do tonight?" she questioned looking around at the setup. "Oh, that's right. Listen, you don't have to…"

"Kaliah, I'd love if you joined me tonight," I smiled feeling super corny but when in Rome you did as the Romans do.

Biting down on her bottom lip again and glared at me over her bouquet of roses. "I would love that."

"Good, because after breakfast you have a spa day set up," I didn't know if it was possible for her to smile any harder than she was. It made me happy to see that I could receive such generosity from her.

"Thank you," her gratitude was refreshing.

"Don't mention it. I couldn't let the day go by without you feeling special," I broke my gaze with her before we gave these innocent bystanders a show.

After breakfast, she stood up from the table and planted a kiss on my cheek before heading towards the spa. With the idle time I took a moment to myself, I walked around property letting my thoughts have their way.

With my seventh season behind me, I was contemplating how much more I really had left in me to give to the NFL. Whatever my next move was had to be a good one. My family depended on me. Mom's medicine had to come every month, and the house had to be paid for each month. Not to mention Ashley, my baby sister, was two years shy of graduation. She needed tuition. Despite my parents telling me not to worry about taking care of home, I had to. Eddie would've knocked me in the chest if I didn't. I owed them everything because without them I wouldn't be.

Finding myself aimlessly walking through the snow I felt my phone buzz in my pocket. Stopping in my tracks, I quickly pulled my phone from my pocket and checked the voicemail from the pilot.

All set to fly out first thing in the morning. We'll send a car for you at noon.

Grinning from ear to ear I was so damn happy to get out of here and get back to civilization. But just as quickly as my smile erupted across my face, it faded. We both knew that this wasn't a forever situation. The Casanova in me wanted this to be forever. Kaliah had some power over me. After one full day together, it was going to be nearly impossible to leave her tomorrow. I had only one night to leave a lasting impression on her that she would compare everything after me to.

Still having some time on my hands to take a nap and rest up for what the rest of my night would hold, I made my way inside. Our last night together had to be a memorable one.

Kaliah James

No man had ever gone out of his way to make me feel as extraordinary as Antonio did today. Others might have

31

thought that this was cliché and minimal, but to me, it meant the world. Especially considering that he didn't have to do a damn thing for me. I didn't need much to be happy. I had everything at my fingertips. Having everything taught me that material things couldn't make you happy. They couldn't fill a void or love you back; you couldn't tell a Gucci bag about your day or your troubles and have it give sound advice in return.

I've talked to Antonio more in these two short days than I've spoken to Alisha in the last few weeks. Even if this didn't go past tonight, I would hold it in my heart forever.

Looking in the mirror at my freshly blown-out hair I nodded in approval before heading up to my room. Alisha was going to scream in sheer excitement when I told her that the dress she packed came in handy. I'd been a homebody when it came to Valentine's Day since my divorce and my mother's passing. Mom and I always made it a point to spend the holidays together. Since she's been gone, I hadn't been in the mood for it much, not until today. I was amazed at what time and healing could do.

Healing had me up in these mountains swooning over a man I was probably never going to see again, ready to risk it all.

Pulling my dress out of the suit bag, I hung it up in the bathroom over the window. Running my hands over the silk material I smirked at Alisha's nerve. This was probably the skimpiest dress I owned. It was a gift from one of my favorite designers and left very little to the imagination.

Sitting at the vanity, I admired my newest edition of red roses. I had the hotel staff put my roses in a vase of water until I departed in the morning. They brought bold color and fragrance to the white marble-encased bathroom.

Pulling my phone out of the drawer, I checked to see if I had enough service to text Alisha.

Two bars. Enough to send a text before getting myself ready for tonight.

I miss you. You'll be proud of me.

Hitting send I put my phone away before applying a sheer layer of makeup to my face.

"Relax, Kaliah," I spoke to myself feeling my hands shake. "It's not like you've never danced with a man before."

True indeed but it'd been so long. What if...

"Okay stop it. Get out your head."

Huffing and tossing my makeup brush down on the vanity, I was searching for every reason not to go through with this. I went back and forth with myself for another ten minutes before hearing my phone buzz. Pulling it out of the drawer to see Alisha's text.

Live your life for right now. Tomorrow is coming with no remorse for yesterday.

She was so poetic at times. Exhaling and looking at my reflection in the mirror. When and where was I ever going to meet another man as equally magical as him? Antonio was rare and whatever woman he ended up with was going to be lucky. I hope she knew that.

5

ANTONIO CLARK

*S*tanding nervously in the lobby waiting for Kaliah to make her grand entrance, I looked at everything but the elevator traveling up and down on its cables. Why I was anxiously waiting on her was just as clear to me as murky water. The same reason that had me ready to bow at her will if she so desired. None of this made sense to me, but I'd be a fool not to go along with it just to see what gold I could find.

I could only pray that she hadn't got cold feet and decided to leave me hanging out to dry. I was looking forward to spending the rest of the night with her. I wanted Kaliah to feel things that no other man had ever made her feel. Desiring to take her to new heights that only we knew about. I felt a burn in my chest every time I thought about leaving her in the morning. I wanted her to know that her sincere investment in me this weekend meant more to me than I could express.

Hearing the elevator doors dig open, I nervously angled my head over my shoulder. Seeing her float off of the elevator in her red dress had my heart and stomach doing somersaults, smirking at the sight of her looking like the chocolate version of Jessica Rabbit. Turning around to face her, I took in the glistening thigh that kept peeking out the split of the dress. She was teasing me. I counted down the moments until I could put my lips on hers.

"I thought you were going to stand me up," I leered down at her while she ran her tiny hands down my black dress shirt. Biting her bottom lip lightly she looked up at me with those enchanting full eyes.

"I thought about it," she admitted. I could feel her unsettled nerves radiate through her body. Snaking my arm around her waist, I lifted her chin with my free hand and placed a soft kiss on her lips.

"Still thinking about it?" I asked after a few more of my kisses landed against her full lips. I've been thinking about doing that since I laid eyes on her my first night here at the bar.

"Not by a long shot," she let out a sultry croon off her lips before taking her hand in mine. Leading her into the ballroom, her eyes danced at the sight of everything. The lights were low, the music was loud enough to vibe to but quiet enough for us to hold a conversation without shouting.

Grabbing two flutes of champagne off one of the trays passing by, I handed her one before escorting her over to an empty table. "What do you want to eat?"

"Surprise me," she smirked seductively while she brought her flute to lips covered in natural tinted gloss. Heading to the different stations to pick out hors-d'oeuvres, I laid my eyes on the chocolate cover strawberries. Catching the attention of a member of the wait staff, I requested a bottle of champagne and some chocolate-covered strawberries to be delivered to my room. Those would come in handy later on tonight. The look in her eyes told me we weren't going to be down here long.

Returning to our high-top table with a few bites to eat, I watched her sway to the music while enjoying what I picked out. Wanting to take in every moment with her I outstretched my hand. Without hesitation, she placed her tiny hand in mine allowing me to lead her to the dance floor.

Wrapping my arms around her body while the band played, we swayed to the music. There wasn't any space between us. I could feel the heat pulsating from her body, and I was sure that she could feel my excitement resting against my thigh. Struggling all day to keep him contained, if she caressed any part of my being again, we were going to make a swift exit to the room.

Listening to her hum Sweet Lady by Tyrese along with the lead singer, I placed a soft kiss on the base of her neck. The way our bodies swayed against each other felt right. Turning her around so her ample ass could rock against my pelvis, she giggled lightly.

While the band continued to sing sultry R&B slow jams my need to feel her flesh on mine grew more. Turning around to look at me she bit down on her thick Hershey bottom lip. She knew exactly was she was doing. "Let's get out of here."

She didn't have to say anymore. Prancing towards the exit, her body lured me to follow her. I became imprisoned under Kaliah's spell. Swaying her hips to and fro to the rhythm of the music, I grunted in anticipation strolling out behind her. I took notice of her shape when we attempted to ski. Her frame supported a set of healthy breasts, hips, and an ass to match. With her love to eat she kept her body in great shape.

Visions invaded my mind while I traveled behind her to the elevator. I wanted to peel that dress from her body and kiss every inch of her brown skin. The entire ride to our floor consisted of my lips caressing exposed parts of her skin. Judging by her moans, she wanted more. Stepping off the elevator, I wrapped her hand in mine. Her hand was so soft against mine. It was trusting in my possession. Leading her into my room, I surveyed the area to make sure they got everything right.

"I don't want to come off like, the only thing I want from you is what you can do for me. Tonight, it's about you. Whatever you want me to do, say the word," I groaned in her ear pulling her body into mine she kissed my jawline lightly. Her kisses were soft. Wherever her lips could touch she kissed. Unbuttoning my shirt, she ran her hands down my chiseled chest.

"Mm," I let a groan escape my throat while she massaged my chest with her tongue and plump lips. Gripping her chin in the palm of my hand I kissed her lips. Opening her lips enough to let my tongue snake in and caress hers I allowed my free hand to explore her body.

Locking her arms around my neck, I backed her up to the window that overlooked the lake. The moon reflected off of the water, creating all the light we needed. Hiking her leg up through the split of the dress I ran my hand up her thigh. only to discover that she wasn't wearing any panties. Squeezing her bare ass in my hand, I broke away and looked down at her.

She was high off our exchange, but she wasn't quite ready for what I was about to do to her body. Stepping away from her I removed my shirt and shuffled my feet over to the chocolate strawberries and champagne. Popping the cork and pouring one glass, I motioned for her to come over. Meeting her in the middle of the floor she welcomed me to place the fruit against her lips. Watching her bite into it while keeping her eyes locked with mine made my dick throb, painfully. Drinking some champagne and covering my mouth with hers she moaned at the explosion of flavor on our tongues. Setting the glass down, I found the zipper to her dress and tugged at it. One tug of the zipper was all it took for the garment to fall to her ankles and I grunted softly at the sight of her bare body with pleasure. She was even more beautiful than I'd imagined.

"You're beautiful," I let out, no louder than a whisper.

Kaliah James

I DIDN'T KNOW WHAT HE WAS DOING TO MY BODY BUT EVERY touch, every kiss left me yearning for more. Whoever taught Antonio how to make love to a woman deserved a Chanel bag and an award. He hadn't even climbed inside yet and I was ready to burst. With my hands pressed against the cold window and my back turned to him, I stood in my heels waiting for him to make his next move. Feeling the cool champagne run down my back, his hot tongue traced it until he reached my ass and bit each cheek causing me to moan. Taking both cheeks in his hand, he grunted while kissing and nibbling them both. The pressure was rising in my center and he was going to make me beg for him. Turning me around to look down at him on his knees, he picked up my leg and held it above his head while his warm mouth latched on to my folds. A deep groan of satisfaction escaped from my depths.

Every move he made was calculated, paced, and passionate. Tightening my core so I wouldn't buckle, he continued to devour me while my river flowed over his face. Our moans took over the room. Inserting his long middle finger into my love caused my back to arch and my breath to quicken. After a few twirls in and out of my honey pot, I pulled his finger out and took it into my mouth while he went back to making love to my flower with his mouth.

"Mmm," he grunted. "You taste better than I imagined."

Pressing my hands against his strong shoulders, I felt myself convulse and drip my appreciation over his face. Standing to his feet, his bulge was more apparent than it was earlier in the night. I wanted - I needed him inside of me painting my walls with his strokes of tenderness. It had been long overdue, and I needed to feel every inch of him.

Now.

Removing himself from his red dress pants, boxers, socks, and shoes, he reached for his wallet and pulled out a gold packet, tearing it open with his teeth. He rolled it over his length and stroked himself a few times before lifting me off my feet. One swift move and he was lowering my body down on his. With my legs wrapped around his waist and his hand pressed against the window, his stroke was unmatched.

My body was getting wetter, my moans were loud, and his husky breath on my neck sent chills all through my body. We were lost in euphoria, and I couldn't speak any words. I didn't want this end. He was taking me places I'd never gone with former lovers.

It wasn't long before he had me bent over the armchair delivering mind-numbing back shots. Feeling my juices drip down my thigh, I was on the edge of an eruption.

Picking my limp body up and laying on the bed he settled back between my body and delivered a series of strokes that caused me to gasp for air and arch my back. Cumming on command with him he grunted, providing the final soul snatching strokes to my kitty before dropping to his back to catch his breath.

"Shit," he blew breathing heavily. "You're not sleeping tonight."

Just as soon as my eyes closed and I began to drift to sleep, I was woken up to his tongue over my swollen pearl. Never mind the sting of our previous session, my body responded to him as if he owned it. He was going to make it so that I could never forget him.

Antonio Clark would be etched in my mind forever.

6

KALIAH JAMES

*T*he sun crept through the window kissing my face with its heat. Sprawled across the bed wrapped I was in his sheets, I knew he was gone. I couldn't feel him. The thought alone made me squeeze my eyes tighter together. I was unprepared to face the reality that Antonio Clark was now a memory. Truthfully, it caused me a great deal of pain to think that it was over. He'd given more than I could ever ask for.

His time.

Sitting my sore body up in the bed I scanned the room rubbing the sleep from my eyes. Images of us in this room flashed in my mind on a slow reel. It made me moan off the recollection alone. That damn Antonio Clark. Closing my eyes, I could still feel his devouring kisses against my skin. Traces of what he did to my body were written all over me. Finding the strength to swing my legs over the edge of the bed, I stood to my feet. Still feeling the soreness between my legs, I would have to suffer through it until I reached L.A. and had time to soak in my tub.

Picking my scattered belongings off of the floor, I trudged

over to my room. My flight was leaving soon, so I had little time to pout over my weekend coming to an end. I went to the Canbury Hotel to reset, and I returned home with so much more than what I was looking for.

After showering and detangling my hair, I dressed my body in the most comfortable outfit I had before packing the rest of my things. Hiking my bags over my shoulder, I rolled my suitcase out the door towards the elevator. Taking in the magic of the third floor once more I felt an involuntary smile creep across my lips. "Magical indeed."

Returning my key to the front desk, I informed the receptionist that I had a room full of roses if anyone wanted them. Reluctantly, I pulled my sunglasses over my eyes as I walked through the front door so the white landscape wouldn't blind me. Seeing my driver from the other day smile and wave at me I started towards him.

"Can I take your bags today, Ms. James?" he smirked as I relinquished them.

"Thank you," I smiled tiredly at him.

There were a few cars lined up waiting for the guests checking out to be chauffeured down the mountain to the airport.

Starting towards the passenger door, I felt an overwhelming presence approach me from behind. I didn't want to turn around because I wasn't sure if my mind was playing tricks on me.

"Kaliah James," his baritone voice caused my center to throb, my heart to flutter, my face to flush and my knees to give a little. Turning to face him, feet sprung to its tiptoes as my arms wrapped around his neck as if they belonged there.

"I thought you left," I hummed as his lips rested against my forehead.

"Not without saying goodbye," he spoke locking eyes with me. "I will never forget you, Kaliah James."

I love how he said my name, how he made me feel, how my body reacted to him like he was home.

Even with all these feelings he'd awakened inside of me, we had an unspoken understanding. This moment was only reserved for right here, right now.

"Me neither, Antonio Clark. Take care of yourself."

Taking my lips in his for one last passionate farewell, we let go of one another grudgingly after a few moments. I couldn't stomach watching him walk away from me, so I broke eye contact with him, swallowed my swelling tears, and climbed into the car. My heart was leaping out of my chest towards him, but I knew in our lives we had no room for each other.

Stuffing my AirPods into my ears, I hit my classic hip-hop playlist and let it take over my senses. I would rather listen to Warren G and Nate Dogg 'Regulate' than some sappy ballads from an artist liable to cause me to break down.

I slept most of the flight back home. I needed it. My body was exhausted from the night before. Dropping my bags by the front door and placing my keys on the counter, I shuffled over to the Bluetooth counsel in the wall dividing the kitchen from the rest of the space in the open floor plan downstairs. Syncing my phone, I let the music play softly throughout the house. Taking a bottle of wine off the rack and a glass out of the cabinet I traveled out of the kitchen. Walking through my living room towards the stairs I looked around at the haze of L.A. through the glass-enclosed lower level.

The view was the reason I fell in love with this home. It was modern and chic and had my name written all over it. The stairs led to a floating loft area that overlooked the lower level. Further down the hall were the bedrooms, four in total. I kept the grey hardwood floors throughout the house. The combination of grey and lavender were settling to me, so I made sure those were two consistent colors throughout my home.

In my bathroom, I leaned over the grey marble tub to fill it with hot water, bath milk, pink Himalayan salt, and dried lavender. Lighting a few candles, I popped the cork on my bottle and poured a glass. I left my phone downstairs so Alisha would have to bother me in the morning. This afternoon, I wanted to relax my aching muscles and sleep before diving back into my chaotic world.

STRETCHING IN MY BED, I PEEKED OVER AT THE CLOCK. IT WAS noon which meant that Alisha was going to be walking through my door at any moment. I gave her a key that she used freely. I didn't mind. Her soft presence always illuminated my home with peace. Pushing my covers off, I slid out of my bed and walked into the closet. Running my fingers over the garments hanging in the closet, I debated on what I wanted to wear. I was partial to leggings and a sweatshirt, but I knew better. Alisha would want to go out on the town to shop, eat, and talk about my trip.

Pulling out my favorite pair of distressed jeans, my camouflage jacket, and a white t-shirt; I took a quick shower and pulled my hair into a messy bun. Zipping my feet into my Louis Vuitton combat boots, I headed down the stairs to find Alisha leaning over my marble countertop intently pecking away at her phone.

"Oh, she lives. I've been calling all morning," Alisha sang not breaking eye contact with her phone. "Only to get here to notice your phone is on the counter and it's dead."

"You missed me, I know you did," I hummed stopping on the other side of the counter. "What's happening in the world today?"

"Well, you have your photoshoot with ELLE tomorrow morning. The call time for that is 6 am so, please be up when I get here. Tomorrow afternoon the script for the new movie comes in. And Andy called, she said she better see you at the gym or she's coming to find you," Alisha rambled off. "But today, you and I are going to stroll around Melrose, get something to eat, and talk about your trip."

Rolling my eyes at the mention of Andy's name. She was going to have to wait until I was done eating my heart out. Grabbing her keys and purse, I followed suit and followed her out the door.

After a couple of hours on Melrose, we were finally eating. Wiggling and swinging my legs underneath the high-top table I hummed while chomping down on my order of truffle fries.

"You're so greedy," Alisha laughed, cutting her eyes at me. "And very happy…"

"I'm always happy when I get food," I shared over a mouth full of fried potatoes.

"No, my love," she whirred her glass in her hands. "That isn't a hungry happy. That's an *I felt it in my soul happy*."

"I don't know what you're talking about, Lish," choosing to ignore the paralyzing memory of Antonio, I shrugged and threw another fry in my mouth.

"You're lying!" she exclaimed. "I know you too well to believe that."

Dragging my eyes into the back of my head, I couldn't begin to deny the power that man had on me. I would run my hand over my bare skin longing to feel his touch again.

"Kaliah Nicole James," Alisha called my entire government name out snapping me out of my thoughts. "Who is this man that has you daydreaming and biting down on your lip like that?"

Inhaling deeply, I looked across the table at her and tried my damnedest not to smile like a little girl in grade school. "I've never met anyone like him in my whole life."

I heard myself gush over him. "What's his name? Where is

he from? What does he do?" her line of questioning made me feel like I was sitting underneath a low light in a cold room.

I wasn't going to tell her his name. Alisha was worse than the FBI. There was no way I was going to give up any information she could use against me. Simply shrugging my shoulders, I clapped my hands when I saw the waitress coming our way with my prime rib burger and Alisha's seared tuna.

"I must admit all I got was his name, which I will never tell you and he might've mentioned that he lives in Philly. What does it matter? It was a mind-blowing one-night stand, and I can promise you I will probably never lay eyes on the man again." Opening my mouth wide to take a bite from the burger that the waitress placed in front of me.

"You little slut," Alisha laughed.

"Yes, yes, I am," I boasted proudly remembering the curve of the monster that commanded my body like it took out a mortgage on it. "And I'd do it again without question."

"You're terrible," she erupted with laughter. "Maybe you should consider getting back into the swing of things."

"Mm, no." Shaking my head from side to side I took another bite.

"So, you can live with a one-night stand, and that's it?"

"Alisha, I have settled with the fact that I will more than likely never marry again," I emphasized *again* so she would understand.

"Daniel was a test drive. We found some screws missing and gave his ass right back to the dealership," she huffed rolling her eyes. Alisha despised him. Given every opportunity to express it she did.

"Could we talk about something else?" I whined not wanting the memory of Antonio to distract me from the juicy burger I held in my hands.

Picking up her phone and reading an email she nodded.

"We sure can. The designer just sent me an email, he moved your fitting up to today so put that burger down."

"I can't even have good things," I whined dropping my burger on the plate. "The minute I'm out that dress I'm calling Uber Eats."

"Andy is going to kick your ass."

7

ANTONIO CLARK

I've been in South Carolina for a whole week and still wasn't able to get Kaliah out of my mind. I found myself staring off into the distance hearing her giggles ring out in my eardrums. Then the flash of her smile caused me to look over my shoulder for her, but she wasn't here. I wanted her everywhere I was. She made me go against everything I thought I believed in. Being with her felt as if I'd been waiting on her all of my life.

"Anton!" Ashley snapped her fingers in front of my face bringing me back to reality. "You don't hear me talking to you?"

"My bad. What's up?" I asked looking up at my baby sister hover over me with her hands on her hips.

"I was asking you about my birthday. You know it's in three days, and you said you'd get me premiere tickets to see My Way Back," she reminded me.

Instantly slapping my forehead, I groaned. I forgot all about it. Between the shit with Jada, my jet, and getting lost in Kaliah for three days, it slipped my mind. "Don't tell me you forgot… I can't believe you forgot Anton!"

Ashley was spoiled, but I had no right to complain about

it because it was at the hand of my own doing. I had to love her twice as hard, for myself and Eddie. "I didn't forget it just slipped my mind."

"Which translates to you forgot. I can't believe you. Jada has your head twisted that bad you forgot about me?" she continued with her scene. "I've only been talking about my sixteenth birthday since my fifteenth."

"Girl, quit," I grunted. "Jada doesn't have nobody's head twisted but her own. I'll get you the damn tickets."

"You better because I told Keisha already and her parents already said yes," she warned plopping down on the couch by me. Pulling my phone out of my pocket I sent a text to my agent. After the trade to Philly, he owed me. If Ashley wanted to be at the premiere of the movie of the year, well damn it she was going to be there even if I had to move hell and high water for her to be there.

Dropping my phone face down in my lap, I looked down at my hands remembering how Kaliah's tiny hands fit into them so perfectly.

"So, if Jada doesn't have your head twisted…who does? You've been staring into space like a sick puppy for since you got home," she announced using her outside voice.

I already told her about finding some damn decorum when she talked to me about my doings. My mother was ready for me to settle down and I wasn't going to give her any false hope.

Kaliah never had to say that what we had wouldn't go on past the Canbury Hotel. I picked it up the night she spoke about her failed relationship. She was too fearful to start something new because her fear of failing was more significant than her cry to be loved correctly. She needed to be loved by someone who heard her heart speak. That night we spent together was more than just a hit and quit for me. I knew she felt that too, the unexplained tears in her eyes communicated what her mouth was too afraid to say.

"Would you mind the business that pays your little intrusive ass?" gritting my teeth I shifted my eyes to make sure my mother was far out of earshot range.

Ashley lost her mind if she thought I was going to tell her about my one-night stand with a woman I barely knew. That would only give her permission to go and be loose in these streets, and I wasn't having that shit.

"Your business pays me," she spoke in a matter of fact tone causing me to roll my eyes.

"You're right, you're right," I nodded my head. "Touché."

Ashley worked at Eddie's Closet better known as EC's throughout the city. It was an athletic apparel store I owned in the Harbison Mall. I left it for my mother to manage and Ashley and her best friend, Keisha to work in. Even though she could get whatever she wanted from me, I had to make sure she understood the value of hard work and the importance of being able to provide for herself. I never wanted my baby sister depending on a nigga for anything. Ashley's independence and self-love were something Eddie, and I spoke about often. All these niggas were about one thing at her age. All they wanted was to bury their little dicks in whatever hole was available. The hole they were in thirsty pursuits for wasn't going to be my baby sister.

Had Eddie been alive he would've been ten times more overbearing than I was. I figured the location monitoring was enough for her to get the hint that even though I wasn't physically present, I was always here. I still kept a watchful eye, and if a little nappy headed ass boy found himself getting too close to her, I was shutting it down off rip.

"So, are you going to tell me?" she continued to pry.

"No, now would you quit?" I asked with force rolling my eyes.

"It's about sex, isn't it? I know about sex Anton so just tell me already," she shared like that information was no big deal. Feeling my caramel skin turn red, I shot my eyes over at her.

49

"How the fuck you know about sex?" I grunted through my teeth.

"Sex ed. Are you stupid? You don't think I'm out here being a little hoeing, do you?" her response settled me enough to relax my core and fall back in the cushions. "Daddy ain't having that shit, and mom has made it very clear that I better not bring anything back in here I didn't leave with. And let's not mention the obvious, you and Eddie were so reckless as teenagers everyone knows you don't play that."

"Good," I smiled at the memory of Eddie and I running around the city like a couple of renegades. "I'm glad my foolish ass behavior can stop you from being stupid behind some dumb ass boy."

"Oh, shut up," she huffed snatching the remote off the coffee table. Growing silent as she flipped the channels she stopped and looked over me. "You ever miss him?"

"Every minute of every day. No one in the world had my back like Eddie did," I shared feeling myself getting emotional. "I wish he was here."

"Me too," she sighed. "All the time. Sometimes, I walk by his room and tap on the door hoping he'll answer. But he doesn't. Then I feel a cool wave come over me. Is that crazy?"

"Nah, that's just Eddie. Reminding us that he's still here," I smirked a little.

The buzzing from my phone saved me from letting a tear go. Sometimes I avoided coming home because it was too much to handle at times. I hated that man who took my brothers' life. For once justice was on our side, and the bastard got life in prison. Still, it didn't bring Eddie back, and it left us with a hole in our hearts we wanted to fill desperately. Football was my outlet, mom and pops had their way of coping with the loss. One was to leave his room exactly the way he left it. The sports posters still adorned the walls, his clothes and sneakers were still in the closet, and his bed was made as if one day he was going to walk back through the door.

Picking up my phone to see a text from my agent informing me that he secured the tickets, I fist pumped the air.

"I got your tickets. I hope you got a dress for this. I don't need your little country ass out in L.A. embarrassing me," I chuckled.

"It's not about you. I just want to go and see Kaliah James. You can get me a dress off of Rodeo or Melrose as a birthday gift," she quipped piquing my interest. I didn't hear anything else she said after Kaliah's name left her lips. I had to play it cool. I didn't need Twitter fingers to my left to get all excited and blow my shit out the water.

"Kaliah James?" I asked pulling my neck back as if I was clueless as to who Ashley was referring to.

"You don't know who she is? Oh my God. I am disappointed," she squealed pecking away at her phone before shoving it in my face. Sure enough, the woman who was consuming my mind was smiling for the cameras in a Getty Images photo. Shit was wild.

"Tell me you can work your magic and I can meet her?" Ashley pleaded. "Please Ton, please."

"Cool out. I'll see what I can do. We're leaving tomorrow, so you and Keisha need to pack your bags. Don't put nothing in there that's going to cause your ass to stay in the hotel room pouting."

"Antonio thank you!" throwing her arms around my neck she squeezed the life out of me. "You're the best brother ever!"

"Yeah, whatever," I chuckled. "Get off me. You got a lot of body heat. Shit makes me itch."

"See, I take it back," she snapped letting me go. "Ma! Help me pack. Anton is taking me to L.A. to meet Kaliah James!"

We both were going to meet the real Kaliah James. Some of us for the first time, others for a third.

She was in the front of my mind again smiling at me. Luring me into her like she'd cast another spell over me. I wasn't even annoyed to find out that she was a movie star. It made things a lot clearer for me.

The life we lived made it hard as hell to find genuine long-lasting friendships, let alone love. I could only help but wonder a few things: was I consuming her mind as much as she was consuming mine? Did she bite down on her lip every time I crossed her mind? Was she as lonely as I was?

It was becoming painfully clear to me that I wanted more from her. I wanted her body and her heart. I just needed the right opportunity for that to take place. I disliked being a man with ulterior motives but if I was going to do a solid for Ashley, she was going to return the favor whether she knew it or not. I had every intention of using her to get me as close as I could to Kaliah.

Picking up my phone to text my agent back, I let him know that I needed to be at whatever party Kaliah was going to be at after the premiere.

We didn't end this in the mountains. It only began.

8

KALIAH JAMES

*R*unning my hands over the front of my floor-length white gown for tonight's movie premiere made me shudder. For a brief second, I imagined that it was Antonio's hands touching me. Since I've been back, I've purposely made myself busy so I wouldn't be tempted to think about his smile, his eyes dancing at me only as they could, and the way he said my name.

I was curious to look him up to see what he was up to. After the curiosity faded, I found myself sighing in relief. I didn't want to know who or what he was up to. I couldn't stomach the thought of him with someone else, doing things to them that he did to me while we were alone, and the moon danced off our brown skin.

Shaking the thought of him out of my head I put my game face on while I looked over my appearance in the full-length mirror. My white dress was simple, but I loved it. I made a mental note to go see Andy in a few days because in my mind I was still on vacation. I was grateful that this dress didn't have any cut-outs. The only skin the was showing was my arms, part of my back, and my cleavage. I wanted something modest, Alisha insisted on having the deep plunge v neck in the front and back of the dress. We compromised deciding on a cut that wasn't so deep. The diamond and emerald choker around my neck glistened under the light along with the teardrop earrings in my ears to match. For a dramatic effect, I threw a violet fur boa over my right shoulder.

My hair was bone straight and flowed like silk. I even had the stylist add in a few extensions for a fuller look. With a deep side part, we brought back the swoop like it was the early 2000's and B2k was still popping. I loved the look. I felt beautiful with the simplicity of it all.

"Are you ready? The car is here," Alisha asked standing in the doorway of my bedroom. She looked equally as beautiful in her royal blue gown. Her short pixie hair cut laid down flat and out of her face while the diamonds I gifted her as a thank you looked terrific against her hazelnut skin.

"You look so pretty!" I smiled, grabbing my gold clutch off my dresser. "You ready to schmooze with these people?"

"The more you schmooze, the more roles you get which keeps both of us employed. Keep it up buttercup," she laughed following me out of the room and down the stairs.

"You should've brought Peter along," I noted collecting my phone and keys and dropping them into my clutch. Killing the lights in the house, I set the alarm before pulling the front door open.

"Peter would rather you let buy him tickets and go sit in the theatre," Alisha smacked her lips at her husband's normalcy. "He's so boring."

"Oh, stop it," I laughed. Peter did not like the spotlight. He would only grace me with his presence if whatever we were doing was either at their house or mine. He told me that watching people run up on me with ease made him anxious. I understood that wholeheartedly which was why I stayed in the house most of the time.

Climbing in the back of the car I tried not to think about Antonio and as hard it was, I tried my damnedest.

When we reached the theatre the line of cars was stretched down the block. As usual, it made Alisha nervous that I was going to miss an interview, a photo, or the chance to shake someone's hand. Personally, I felt it all was unnecessary. I was an actress, not the Pope, it didn't matter whether or not I shook a hand, took an interview or a picture. My work should've spoken for itself. However, we lived in a world where the more you shared, the more relevant you became.

Alisha was pecking away on her phone again which only meant she was texting someone who knew something about the wait. "Lishaaa," I whined placing my hand on her phone and pushing it into her lap. "Please, stop. Let's just enjoy tonight, please?"

"Kaliah," she blew causing me to wave my finger.

Feeling the car creep down the road, I smiled at her. "Fine. I'll give it a break. But don't give me a look when something starts happening and you need me to handle it."

"We're going to have a good night," I finalized. It was going to be a long night, and the last thing I wanted was Alisha to be up in arms over me. Tonight, she was my plus one, I wanted her to enjoy herself.

Finally, walking on the red carpet, Alisha stuck by my side. I loved having her here, it helped me focus on work instead of consuming myself with the likes of Antonio's very meddling memory.

"You are doing great!" she whispered in my ear as we started in towards the theatre. "You're going to have them eating out your hand after this."

"My cheeks are burning," I blew turning my face to her to drop my smile for a second. "When we get in here, I'm getting some nachos and Mike and Ike's."

"You're thinking about food, again?" Alisha chuckled as if my desire for food was something new to her. "You barely made it into the dress."

"Speaking of which-" I started my statement and lost all thought and will to continue to speak.

Looking over Alisha's shoulder my attention was drawn to a familiar glare that caused my heart to cease its beating. Everything around me came to a crashing halt. I didn't care about the cameras or reporters calling my name. Consumed in a trance, I found my feet gliding through the crowd to meet him halfway.

My eyes traced over his body, taking in how handsome he was in his perfectly tailored navy-blue suit paired with a grey and blue plaid vest and a paisley tie. He looked so good, and the sight of him made my center pulse.

"Kaliah James," his baritone vibrated in my eardrums wrapping his arms around my waist, pulling me into a hug.

"Antonio Clark," I swallowed the lump in my throat and inhaled his scent.

"You owe me," he whispered in my ear.

By now I was sure all the cameras were catching every bit of our interaction. Nothing mattered at the moment but Antonio Clark. "The thought of you has been consuming me."

I could admit the same, but I'd rather just stand here and take in his hypnotizing scent. For a brief second, I forgot about Alisha until she started calling my name.

"Kaliah," Alisha gritted through her teeth. "Kaliah James! They are watching you!"

"Antonio, they're seating us." I heard a soft voice join in with Alisha's grunts.

"Ashley, you didn't tell me that your brother knew Kaliah James. From the looks of it, he *really* knows her. You feel me?" another feminine voice came into earshot.

Letting him go, I stepped back looking at every reporter, photographer, and guest alike within ten feet as they stared at our exchange. Not only were they soaking up all this potential gossip, but Alisha and a pair of young ladies were watching as well.

"Annntonnniiiioooo," the whining continued causing me to draw my eyes away from him and to the teenage girl standing to his right. Once she looked at me her face lit up. "You didn't tell me you knew Kaliah James!"

She shrieked excitedly before jogging in place then pulling me into a joyous hug. "I can't believe it is really you!"

Chuckling at how excited she was, I couldn't help but engage her. Her outward expression was exactly what was going on inside of me. She was excited to see me, and I was excited to see Antonio.

"Excuse the crazy it's her birthday, and she doesn't get out much," Antonio smiled not taking his eyes off of me. "This is my baby sister Ashley and her best friend, Keisha."

"It's so nice to meet you ladies," I replied feeling Alisha tug on the boa hanging over my shoulder after I greeted Keisha with a hug. "And this is my best friend Alisha who doubles as my assistant and publicist."

"Kaliah, we have to get in our seats," Alisha pushed. Cringing at the thought of leaving him again, I finally acknowledged Alisha's pushiness.

"Okay," I blew. "You three can come and sit with us."

Ashley and Keisha jumped at the opportunity and pulled Antonio by the arm into the theatre with Alisha and me.

"Who the hell is that?" Alisha grunted in my ear. "Tell me that's not the guy from the mountains."

"Alisha, could we not do this right now?" I whispered back while we were ushered into the theatre.

"If you think I'm going to let this go, you're wrong. We're going to wake up to a PR storm tomorrow," rolling my eyes into my head Alisha had gone from my best friend to publicist within seconds. These were the times I wished I would've actually hired one who I could ignore. The scowl on her face told me she wasn't letting go of this any time soon. It was one thing for me to fly off and meet a stranger I'd never see again. It was another when the stranger was present, all she could think about was my brand and ultimately my heart.

"Oh boy," I groaned before taking my seat next to Antonio and his sister.

Once I settled down from Alisha's disapproval of being blindsided by Antonio, I found my mind taking flight. I spent every minute of the premiere thinking about ditching the after-party and spending my night with Antonio. With the fit Alisha just had I knew that would be damn near impossible.

Feeling my phone buzz in my clutch I pulled it out and glanced down at the screen. Cutting my eye towards the end of the aisle, Alisha placed her cell back in her lap and focused her attention on the screen, again. *"We're ditching the after-party. Peter has reservations at the Water Grill. He wants to meet your friend."*

9

KALIAH JAMES

*S*ince my mother passed Alisha conveniently filled her spot with ease. I appreciated how much she cared about my well-being, so I let it ride most of the time. She knew when she was overdoing it. This dinner was only an olive branch to undo the irritation and have Peter pick up where she left off.

"Kaliah, that movie was amazing," Ashley gushed placing her hand over her chest. "Girl, I got all the feels."

My Way Back was my fourth screen feature. My career took off like a rocket after my second feature, and there wasn't any stopping in sight, but I was still humble. After all, I was still a small-town girl from Alabama who just happened to get her big break.

"Don't do that," I blushed. "Since it's your birthday how about you join us for dinner?"

"Are you serious!? Uh, hell yes!" she exclaimed grabbing Keisha's hand in excitement. Catching Alisha's eye, I smiled and mouthed thank you.

Nodding her head, she turned and walked towards the exit. Like second nature Antonio grabbed my hand and led me through the crowd towards the door behind Alisha.

Arriving at the restaurant, we settled around the table after the greetings were done. I still hadn't gotten around to exactly what it was that Antonio did that got him here. Honestly, I didn't care. He was here with me.

"Antonio, what brings you here from Philly?" Peter asked looking across the table at Antonio intently. Peter could size someone up with one conversation alone.

"The weather," he chuckled. "That and Ashley wasn't going to let me go back home without bringing her out here to celebrate her birthday."

"How old are you?" Alisha asked Ashley after taking a sip from her wine glass.

"Sixteen," Ashley smiled enjoying her bread and butter. "There was no way I was spending my sixteenth birthday in South Carolina."

"Happy birthday," Peter smiled kindly at Ashley. "However, the question that's still on the table is how do you two know each other?"

"Yeah, that part," Ashley and Keisha said in unison.

"Alright, double mint twins," Antonio chuckled shaking his head.

"My brother has no game whatsoever. I need to know this story," wiping her hands on the cloth napkin covering her lap she rested her chin on her fist. "Don't spare any details."

"This is why I don't take your ass out the house," Antonio continued to shake his head with a grin exposing those beautiful teeth. "Would you like to share? Or have me do the honors?"

The thought of having to sit here in front of Alisha, Peter, Ashley, and Keisha telling them the story of how I knew Antonio for two days before I was bent over busting it open gave me anxiety.

"Go for it," I hummed into my wine glass.

"Alright so boom," he started making both Keisha and

Alisha giggle while Ashley and Peter shook their heads amused before he could start the story.

"Here we go, it's about to be a whole lot of lying," Ashley rolled her eyes. "Mark my words."

"Have some faith in your big brother, would you?" Antonio smirked placing his hands on his chest. "So, my jet had some issues, and we had to make an emergency stop in Montana. The closest hotel from where we landed was the Canbury. I spotted her while I was eating dinner, we had a little exchange on the elevator-"

"A little exchange?" I questioned drawing my neck back and pinning my brows together. "Tell them the truth, you were irritated and took it out on me."

"But I made up for it, didn't I?" he questioned looking me over with those eyes.

"You did," remember those two days and the night to close it out. "You did."

"Nothing else to it. Honestly, I thought I was never going to see Kaliah again," Antonio shared scanning over the group.

"Let me get this right," Peter started raising an eyebrow looking at us. "You went the whole weekend without knowing who Kaliah was?"

"Not a shred. Alisha made sure the hotel staff kept who I was to themselves, and I wasn't glammed up at all," I admitted.

"I just kept my head down until I saw Kaliah," Antonio's eyes danced when they landed on mine. Taking my hand in his and bringing my knuckles to his lips, I bit my lip lightly thinking about those lips.

"From the looks of it, y'all going to be seeing a whole lot more of each other," Keisha giggled.

"Right?" Ashley chimed in. "Wait until I tell mommy this."

"Mind the business that pays you, little girl," Antonio's

words caused Ashley to cut her eyes and smack her eyes at him.

Chuckling, Peter smiled at the two of us. I hadn't brought anyone around him since Daniel. His reaction to Daniel wasn't nearly as pleasant as this. I should've known back then that Daniel would've been hell to deal with by Peter's response alone.

The rest of the evening went well, Alisha came around as Antonio sparked up a conversation with her about random topics. Just because she was coming around doesn't mean that she was completely sold yet.

"You should've let me pay for dinner," I whined as he pulled me in his arms on the other side of the car Alisha and I took to get here. Standing out of the view from the street, I laid my head on his chest. The chill of the night mixed with his warmth made this moment perfect.

"Stop it," feeling his chest vibrate against my ear, I sighed. "Where's your phone?"

"In my clutch," responding and lifting my head off his shoulder. Pulling it out of my clutch in one swift move, he took it from between my fingers into the palm of his hand. Entering his number, he placed it back in my hand and kissed my forehead.

"I'm going to get these two back to the hotel. When you get home send me your location," licking those full lips, I wasn't focused on anything but the feel of them on my skin. Nodding my head, I stepped back letting him go completely. Turning to climb into the back seat of the car, he tucked the minimal train of my dress into the car. "I'll see you soon."

ANTONIO CLARK

Antonio Clark

"Where do you think you're going?" Ashley sassed, placing her hand on her hip standing next to Keisha whose arms rested in front of her body.

"To see his girlfriend," she chimed. Both of them were annoying, and part of me regretted traveling across the country with two teenage girls who thought they knew every damn thing.

"Don't come back with nothing you didn't leave with," Ashley mocked our mother's famous words. "I know it's Kaliah James and all but still."

"I swear, I am never taking you two nosey asses anywhere else. Y'all have no home training whatsoever."

"Mm," Ashley pressed her lips together followed by an eye roll. "So, you're just going to leave us here alone to go bump some skins."

"Where are you getting this shit from?" I asked looking at her. This was the third reference she made to sex, and I was now looking at her crazy. "Listen, mind your business little girl. Don't y'all leave this hotel, don't get into no shit, and leave the mini-bar alone. Order whatever you want from room service."

"Anything?" they asked in unison forcing my eyes to roll again.

"I'm just curious 'cause the restaurant had them little plates, and I'm still hungry," Keisha shared plopping down on her bed.

"Whatever you want," bouncing my eyes from both of them. I pointed my finger at the pair. "No shit."

"Alright, Anton. Go be with your girlfriend," Ashley shooed me away.

Shaking my head, I turned to walk towards the door. Stopping and looking over my shoulder at the two of them. "We know, no shit."

"And if y'all bump into a nigga name Robert Kelly, run away."

Making that my final statement I walked across the hall to my room and grabbed my duffle bag. Heading towards the elevator, I checked my phone to see Kaliah's address followed by a heart emoji. Returning the energy, I slipped my phone into my pocket.

There's never been a time in my life where I was this open over a woman. But Kaliah, she was different. It didn't bother me that she was a star. I could've cared less. The woman I met in the mountains of Montana was easy going, down to earth, and had an unmatched sense of peace surrounding her. I needed that in my life. She was capable of being a bad habit that I welcomed with open arms.

My nerves were unsettled. They were like carbonated water building up pressure in a bottle. The minute the seal broke they were going to erupt. The entire ride to Kaliah's home consisted of me running my hands over my suit pants. When I saw her float down the red carpet in her white gown,

I felt the air from my lungs become trapped. She made my world stop. My entire body locked up. Once our eyes connected, it was a jolt of energy that restarted everything. I knew that whatever we had going was more than just a night under the moon.

Feeling the car stop in front of her large oak trimmed doors, I cleared my throat and pulled myself out of the back seat with my duffle bag. Thanking the driver, I headed up her steps and rang the doorbell. I was anxious, and it was annoying. Every time I was in her presence, I didn't feel like myself, it felt as I was being molded into something better than who I was. The feeling was indescribable. What I knew was I didn't want to let her go again.

After a couple of moments of waiting at her front door the heavy oak door with the smoky windows pulled open. Standing in front of me, she was beautiful. Kaliah looked like the first night I laid eyes on her. Kaliah's natural face glowed under the light of the front porch. Her hair was pulled into a high bun exposed her beautiful chocolate face.

"Hey," she beamed stepping back and letting me into her home. Giving her a once over I saw she was comfortable in a black tank top, Nike shorts, and a silk robe hanging over her arms.

We could talk later. Right now, I wanted to be buried deep inside of her with her nails digging into my skin. Closing the door behind us, I dropped my bag by the front door and pulled her into my arms.

KALIAH JAMES

The way he kissed me had my body ready to react off that alone. Standing in the foyer of my home with his sloppy kisses covering my lips was what I'd been thinking about since I left him in the mountains. Our tongues wrestled while he placed his hand on my neck. Keeping his lips wrapped around mine, his strong hand traveled from my neck to my breast. Massaging one through my tank top made a moan escape from my mouth into his. Pulling away and biting down on his lip, he backed me into the kitchen.

With my waist pressed against the countertop, he took my lips back between his. My lips, chin, neck, and earlobes were covered with his kisses. I was high off of them. In the same token, I was being tortured. The heat he was causing to rise between my thighs was now becoming uncomfortable. I wanted him inside coating my walls while I covered him.

"I missed you," he whispered in my ear making the tiny hairs all over my body to stand straight up. "You've kept me up every night I was away from you. You owe me."

Running my hand over his shoulders to remove his suit jacket, I bit down on my bottom lip and looked up at him seductively. "I'm sorry."

"You're not sorry, yet," he hushed me with a smack to the ass before lifting my body and sitting me on the counter. Spreading my legs open with his body, he slipped my robe off my shoulders and removed my tank. Taking my swollen breasts into his mouth, he sucked, kissed, and nibbled on each of my nipples drawing moans out of me. "You are going to pay for every night I had to be without you."

Gliding a hand into my shorts, he found my pearl and grinned at how wet I was. "You missed me, I see."

"I did," I moaned while he worked his index and middle finger in a circular motion. Feeling him slide a finger inside I gasped and arched my back. "Anton..."

"You didn't give this away, did you baby?" he asked working another finger in and out of me. I was trying to stay focused, but it was so hard. Shaking my head, no, between moans I could see him smile in satisfaction from underneath my hood eyes.

With his free hand, he pulled the hair tie from my hair, letting my high bun unravel and my hair fall over my shoulders. "Good. This is mine."

"Okay," I moaned. My defenses were down, and I was on the cusp of an explosion.

"Not yet," he smirked pulling his fingers out and placing them in his mouth and sucking my juices off his fingers. "You taste so damn good."

Letting our mouths collide again, I got a taste of myself, while he tugged my shorts down. Stepping back, he pulled them completely off and tossed them on the floor. "Lay back," he directed placing a leg over each shoulder, I did as I was told. I was unable to resist his advances; my body was his.

Burying his face between my face, he kissed my jewel. It was wet, sloppy and I could hear him smacking and slurping as if dinner wasn't enough and dessert was being delayed. Holding my breasts in my hands, I squeezed my nipples while he was trying to pull an eruption from my core.

Reaching up, he moved my hands out the way and took over. My moans mixed in with his and the sounds of my wetness filled my kitchen.

Right as I was about to erupt, he stopped and stood up with a devilish smirk on his face. "You're torturing me," whining with my back pressed against the marble counter I stared at the ceiling hearing his pants unzip. Sitting up I started to unbutton his shirt while his belt hit the floor.

"It'll be worth it," he hummed as I began to kiss his neck. Trailing kisses from his neck to his chest, I slid my body off of the counter down to my knees. Taking him into my hands, I started to massage his rod while juggling his balls with my other hand. If he was going to play this game, so was I. He was just as responsible as I was for the anguish he's caused in his absence. Grunting, he rested his palms against the counter while I took his length into my mouth. Wrapping my mouth around him tightly, I started sucking him as my life depended on it. The taste of his precum on my tongue was making my kitty throb with anticipation.

Antonio was trying to control himself, but it was evident that I had him wrapped around my pinkie. Kissing the tip and resuming my bob, I gripped his hips to steady my motion. Looking up at him, I saw him bite down on his lip trying to gather himself. He was close to letting himself go and tried his best to hold on. Giving him a few more bobs I let him go and stood up.

"You've been on my mind too," I whispered pressing my nose against his. "I touch myself imagining it's you."

Engulfing me in his arms, he picked me up, and legs automatically wrapped around his waist. Feeling his manhood pressed against my aching honey pot, I lightly bit down on his shoulder.

"I want all of you or nothing," I made my intentions clear. It was clear to me even under this haze of ecstasy I wanted Antonio Clark more than one night. "Can you provide that?"

"Kaliah James, I cannot go a day without you," his husky voice in my ear made me wetter. Pushing his hardness into my soft folds made me gasp for air and hold on to him tightly.

He paralyzed me, I couldn't say any more. I held on as tight as I could while he traveled up the stairs with me wrapped around him.

"Third door to the right," I moaned directing him to my bedroom.

Entering the room, he laid me on my back and began to stroke my walls hitting my spot. "Is that it?"

Nodding my head while I bit down on my lip trying not to let my sounds of pleasure go. I wanted to hold on to them a little while longer.

"Let that shit go. I love hearing your moans," Antonio groaned in my ear. "Shit."

Releasing my melodic moans in his ear, I wrapped my body around him as tightly as I could. I loved the feel of his skin against mine. If we could be any closer, I would welcome it. Feeling my body release and coat him, it only gave him the motivation he sought to dive deeper to coax more eruptions from my core. Everything he set out to get he did. I cried his name while digging my nails into his back. Soon, he painted my walls with his seeds and let a loud groan that vibrated against my ears.

Laying on my side with my leg wrapped around his, my head rested on his arm as I admired his caramel face underneath the night light shining through my window.

"What's on your mind?" he asked brushing my hair out of my face.

"I don't want this to end," I admitted hating the idea of him leaving again.

"It's not," he shared. "If you think I'm letting you walk away from me a second time, you're out your mind. So, Kaliah James...tell me about yourself."

Laughing lightly, "We definitely skipped that step, didn't we? I'm 29. My birthday is on October 20th. I'm a professional actress, I've been married once. It was a failure.

As you already know, I love to eat, and I can shop like I get paid to do it. I need you to understand that I have my own means to get whatever I want, the only thing I require from you is honesty and love, eventually. Fortunately, for you, you've met my family. Alisha is my best friend, sister, personal assistant and sometimes she thinks she my mom."

"How does your mom feel about that?" he chuckled.

"I'm sure she's happy that she left me in good hands. She passed away a couple of years ago from lung cancer. I never knew my father and mom was estranged from her family because of my father. He moved her from Virginia to Alabama and left her when she told him about me. No one has seen or heard from him since. She was stubborn and refused to go back home, so she made a life for us there. She did a damn good job too. So, Alisha and Peter are my constants."

"I'm sorry about your mom. I know how it feels to lose someone close to you. I lost my older brother to an argument at a gas station over a pump. I will never forget that night, I close my eyes sometimes and feel him. My parents live in Lexington, South Carolina, they'll probably never move as long as Ashley is content. I travel home as much as my schedule allows," he shared. "I'm 30, my birthday is April 8th. I'm a free safety in the NFL. I play for Philly, and I hate the weather. The only thing I want from you is you. All of you, the good parts, the ugly parts, and the pieces of yourself that you hide away from the world. Also, I'm a homebody."

"I'm sorry about your brother, I couldn't imagine," I sympathized with him.

"It gets better with time."

"Despite what you might believe, I hate the spotlight, and

I'd rather be home in a t-shirt reading a book or watching National Geographic," I replied with a yawn.

"I don't think we're going to have any issues," kissing my forehead. "Go to sleep. I'll be right here when you wake up."

Snuggling into his chest, I drifted off to sleep.

Antonio Clark

WAKING UP TO THE SOUND OF THE DOORBELL I LOOKED OVER AT Kaliah who was stretched out underneath the covers snoring lightly. Grunting, I got up and jogged down the stairs. Opening my bag up and digging some shorts out I pulled them over my body before cracking the door open. Seeing Ashley and Keisha standing on the other side of the smoked glassed door with slick smiles on their faces sent irritation through my being. I remember telling them not to pull any shit.

"What the hell are you two doing?" cocking my head to the side, I knew there was a reason they were here. "Did y'all get kicked out of the hotel?"

"Kicked out is a bit extreme don't you think?" Keisha smirked. "Invited to leave is more like it."

Palming my face, I looked over my shoulder to see Kaliah, and I's mess from the night. I quickly closed the door and picked up our clothes off the floor and stuffed them in my duffle bag. I didn't want to give Ashley or Keisha any ammunition. It was already bad enough that I was going to have to call the hotel and figure out the damage if any.

"I got the rest of your stuff," Ashley smiled opening the door. "This is nice."

"I know, she's rich, rich," Keisha popped her gum nodding looking at the open floor plan of the first level. The sight of these two annoyed the hell out of me. There went my plans to be buried inside of Kaliah before breakfast.

"Do either one of you have plans on telling me how you got here and why?" I asked leaning my back on the counter with my arms folded across my body.

"Well, we may have been running up and down the halls, and security was called on us. And you forgot that you shared your location with me. I always know where you are," Ashley smirked waving her phone in the air. "So, what's for breakfast?"

I was going to knock her happy ass into a wall.

KALIAH JAMES

$\mathcal{T}$he light sounds of giggles flowed up the stairs into the crack of my bedroom waking me up. Squinting my eyes over towards the clock on my nightstand, I yawned and forced my sore body out of bed. Walking into the bathroom I surveyed the passion marks Anton left on my body from the night before. As sore and worn out as my body was, I wanted it again. By far he was the best lover I'd ever have.

After taking a quick shower, I headed down the stairs to see Ashley, Keisha, and Anton seated around the counter. Someone ordered breakfast, I knew they didn't get that spread from my kitchen. I barely cooked most of the time. Glancing over at the three of them I noticed the pensive look on Antonio's face.

"Good morning," I greeted the three with a smile.

"Saved by the bell!" Keisha cheered throwing her hands up in the air.

"Please, explain to my caveman of a brother that it's perfectly fine for me to entertain a few guys at once," Ashley rolled her eyes and folded her arms over her chest.

"Sorry, I didn't want to wake you up. These two clowns

got kicked out of the hotel," Antonio shared pulling me into a hug.

"Well," I chuckled catching Antonio's side eye after he covered my lips with a kiss. "It depends on what context of entertaining we're talking about…"

"Well?" Antonio asked jerking his head back.

"Calm down," I laughed at his dramatization. "She's young, entertaining could be a conversation."

"Or it could be something else. I'm a man, I know what men want. When I was sixteen, I was a hoe, Ashley. I'm telling you these little niggas are going to make me hurt them," he blustered scowling his face while the three of us rolled our eyes.

"Dare I ask how we got on this conversation?" scanning over the two they shook their head no with an eye roll.

"Normal Anton. Different day," Keisha sighed.

"Hm," he huffed. "At least I care about your fast little asses."

"Babe," I sang. "Let it go."

"Babe?" Ashley smirked. "So y'all official, official?"

"What's it to you?" Antonio asked giving her a hard time.

"Uh, that you're dating someone we actually like and the fact that that's Kaliah James. What you mean what's it to me?" scoffing, she flicked a piece of paper in his direction. I loved the bond these two had. I had siblings on my father's side I never met, and I was unsure if I would ever meet them. I remember being Ashley's age and wanting someone to look out for me the way Anton did her.

"Yes, Jada was a piece of work. I'm happy to see you've upgraded your standards," Keisha chimed in while I picked up a plate and started fixing my food.

"Well, damn just lay my shit bare," he groaned leaning on the counter looking over the three of us.

"I'm going to tell her everything. Wait until mom and dad get a hold of her," Ashley grinned.

"Hold up," Anton blew shaking his head and held his hand up in protest. "They will not get their hands on anyone."

"Yeah, we'll see about that," she giggled.

Not paying much attention to his comment, I looked over at Ashley and Keisha then their bags by the front door. I liked them and having entertaining company was welcomed. I was sure after getting kicked out of their hotel that Antonio was not going to let them out of his sight. "So, I have three guest bedrooms you two can choose from. Since you didn't have an actual party last night let's have one today."

Seeing her face brighten from my suggestion made my heart smile. "Are you serious?"

"Yeah, and if your brother doesn't have any plans for tomorrow, I'll take you sightseeing," I smiled as Antonio moved around the counter, resting his chin on my shoulder and wrapping his arms around my waist.

"You don't have to do that," he hummed against my eardrum.

"You'll learn quickly that I do what I want. Plus, I like them, and it makes no sense that she's sixteen in L.A. and not enjoying it," I pointed out while Ashley and Keisha engaged in their social media.

"You're going to be a problem," kissing the base of my neck.

"I am a good problem."

The more time I spent with Antonio the closer I was drawn to him. Not only was he sexy as hell and a monster in the bedroom but his sense of self and family background filled something in me that I didn't know I was missing. Sure, part of me missed that my father wasn't around and giving his other children something, he never gave me, but it never really mattered to me much. The more energy I gave it, the more it nagged me. There were periods where I hated him. Daddy-daughter dances, he wasn't there. Homecoming, prom, graduation; he wasn't there. My first heartbreak, he wasn't there. With my divorce and my mother dying, his ass was nowhere to be found. I found myself continually making excuses for his inability to father.

I played out all of the scenarios in my head. I even gave him every excuse in the book, maybe he wasn't ready to be a father. According to my mother, he had a daughter a year after I was born. So, it was just me he couldn't love. I was the only one he failed.

"Kaliah," Anton's voice droned in my ear while I cleaned up the kitchen from breakfast. "You good?"

Forcing a smile across my face, I nodded. I wasn't good, but there would be a day where I stopped wanting my father to be a father. "Uh," he blew. "I know enough to know…talk to me."

Tossing the container with the left-over eggs in the trash, I glanced over at Ashley and Keisha hanging outside by the pool with their feet in the water. They were happy. The sixteen-year-old me would've killed to be that calm and protected.

"I'm watching how you two interact, and I can't help but be jealous. I would've killed to have someone look after me like that when I was sixteen. I never thought it bothered me until right now. My father has five other kids, and he's active in all their lives, and he just left me," my brows pinned together, and felt myself getting emotional. "I'm sorry."

"Why are you apologizing?" his intense eyes beamed down at me. "You have nothing to be sorry for. The only one who should be sorry is him for leaving you. In all honesty, it's his loss. You turned out dope as hell without him."

"Why are you so amazing?" I asked feeling my cheeks turn hot.

"I'm just Antonio, baby. You'll learn that I don't care where you been, who you've been with or what you've done, I'm not going anywhere," I swear his words were silk and if we didn't have company, I would give him a replay of last night right here.

"You sure about that?" I asked raising my brow while he planted himself in front of me, instantly biting down on my lip I looked into his face.

"I get you've been with some losers, but it only takes a real man a few hours to know what he's dealing with. From there he determines whether or not it'll be worth it. You're worth it, and I'll do whatever I have to for you to remember that."

Locking his lips around mine, I got lost in his kiss.

"Ahem," the sounds of giggles floated over his broad shoulders.

"I swear their asses are going to be on the first thing smoking," he grumbled stepping back and looking over his shoulder. "What?"

"You've had her all night. Can we have her now?" Ashley asked.

Holding his hands up in the air he turned around and leaned on the counter. "It's your birthday weekend."

Joining the girls around the pool, I looked over my shoulder making sure Antonio was out of earshot range. "I want to know about these boys."

Before I knew it, I was engulfed in the high school gossip that Ashley and Keisha served piping hot.

Antonio Clark

KALIAH HAD ME WIDE OPEN. SO MUCH SO I WAS ABOUT TO TELL her I loved her had Ashley not interrupted. I was glad she did. Uncertain of what this woman was doing to me, I knew that being apart from her let alone moving forward without her was now out of the question. My intentions with her had to be made clear, and before I left, I was going to do so.

The three of them had been bonding since breakfast and I wasn't even attempting to get a word in. Ashley never took to anyone this fast. It probably helped that Kaliah was someone she looked up to. My heart swelled watching them interact, almost as if she was family already. Hearing the door open, I looked over my shoulder at Alisha and Peter walking in with balloons, bags of food, and cupcakes. Standing up to help, I caught a look of disapproval on Alisha's face.

"What's up, big man?" Peter greeted with a hand slap after we placed everything on the counter.

"Chilling. Hey Alisha," I smiled as she trotted away.

"Mhmm," was all I managed to get from her as she walked outside towards the pool.

"Don't pay no mind to her. She's protective," Peter chuckled shaking his head.

"Understandably so," I nodded slowly. "I'm not trying to take Kaliah for a ride or nothing like that."

"Believe me, I know. You're the most stand-up guy that's stepped to Kaliah, ever. Lisha just doesn't want her heart-broken again. Because if you leave, she's going to be here picking up the pieces," Peter shared glancing over at me.

He was sizing me up, and I was cool with that. I knew how this went. Kaliah already had a life set up without me, I was entering in on a scene that was already reeling. "Can I be real with you for a second without you looking at me crazy?"

"What's up?"

"Front the moment I laid eyes on her, I knew that she was going to be someone I didn't want to live without. I've never been big on love at first sight or rushing into something, but man," I blew feeling like I was having an out-of-body experience.

"You don't have to tell me twice," laughing he looked at his wife as if he was falling in love all over again. "The moment I saw that woman, I knew that she was mine. She played hard to get, but Kaliah ran interference for me. I haven't backed up off her since."

"I'm in good company."

"All I ask is that you do right by her."

"I got you."

Ashley was enjoying every moment of this and Kaliah was going right along with my sister's obsessive behavior. Times like these were when I was thankful that Ashley had a great personality because she comes off as crazy. She definitely took after Eddie and pops with that one. However, I would be lying if I said I wasn't obsessed with Kaliah my damn self.

"You're drooling," Alisha's voice startled me. "I really need to be clear on your motive with my best friend."

"What do you mean? There's no motive," I shared looking down at her. Alisha wasn't any taller than Kaliah, but by the way, she talked you would think that she was a six-foot-seven-inch man with built up aggression. When she was talking to Peter or Kaliah, her demeanor changed.

"So, you two have a little thing in the mountains, and you're here now. What're your intentions with Kaliah? She's taken by you, and it scares me. When Kaliah falls in love, she forgets about herself and consumes herself with whoever it is at the moment. I fear that you can't love her the way she'll end up loving you," Alisha spoke plain. "Her love is crazy intense, and it's real-life in your face all day every day. She is the only person I know that gives love that hard."

The love and protection she and Peter carried for Kaliah were great. If they only know that I wanted to take a piece of that responsibility for myself.

Amused by her comment, I shook my head. "Why can't I have the capacity to love her?"

"Men like you don't love anyone but yourselves. I see how you athletes parade around like you're God's gift to the earth. The fact that you can smash your body into someone else keeping them from catching a ball means nothing to me. I care about you handling my friend with care," she continued. Alisha formed an opinion of me in her mind that was the exact opposite of who I was.

"Men like me?" I couldn't help but laugh at her statement and shake my head.

"Did I say something amusing?" she cocked her head to the rose her eyebrow.

"Nah, but you're funny to assume that all of us are the same. Everything you said regarding me is wrong. If I wanted someone to fuck, I would've gone for that. It's not hard to find a woman with no morals to bend over. That's just real talk. Kaliah ain't that woman. You know that for yourself. I've heard that her past lovers weren't shit, but I can guarantee you that my mom and pops didn't raise a man who wasn't about nothing. I know quality when I see it. If I had any other intentions besides to do her right, I would've stepped off. You got me penned all wrong," breaking it down so it could forever be broken, Alisha closed her mouth and raised her brow.

"Are you a mythical creature?"

"Nah, just Antonio Henry Clark from Lexington, South Carolina," I smiled. "Alisha, Kaliah is in good hands."

"I'll be the judge of that. Be good to her, she deserves that much."

KALIAH JAMES

J was supposed to getting ready to take Ashley and Keisha shopping on Rodeo Drive, but instead, Antonio had my legs wrapped around his waist, my arms locked around his neck while moaning his name seductively in his ear. The hot water shooting from the dual shower heads beat our backs as we consumed ourselves with each other. I had several things to be upset about, one was the fact that we had company waiting and the other was my hair was drenched.

"Anton," I moaned. "Baby, I got to goooo."

"They can wait," he whispered placing his lips on my neck. He was quickly learning my spots, and my neck was one of them. He was opening the floodgates and making me reconsider staying in the house today with him and just sending the girls off to do their thing.

Feeling him hit my spot, I wrapped myself around him tighter. "Shit."

It wasn't long until my juices coated him, and he pulled out, shooting his seeds down the drain. Lowering my legs to the tile floor of the shower I held on to him to steady my shaking. "We're going to fight."

"Why? Because I got your hair wet?" he asked running his hands through my natural curls and kissing my lips. "I love it. You look beautiful."

"Stop before I don't leave this room," I smiled slapping his chest and turning the water off. Stepping out of the shower and grabbing my towel I covered my body.

"Would that be a bad thing?" he asked stepping out behind me not taking his eyes off me. I could feel them glaring at me with my back turned to him. "You do know that I'm not going anywhere, right?"

"Well, I assumed after the other night that we were doing something. Was that a correct assumption?"

"It was," nodding and standing by me at the sink. "I need you to understand that what I feel for you is more than sex. There's not a part of you that I don't want."

Looking over at him, he held my stare. My heart dropped, my brain told me to run. We've been down the road of falling in love before, and we knew the outcome. However, everything I thought I knew about love changed the minute Antonio walked into the hotel. "Are you falling in love with me?"

I needed to know. I could live with whatever answer he gave. It was better to know right now than to hear later down the road that this wasn't love but a haze of euphoria.

"I already fell," sharing his fate with me we stood in silence. "Never in my life have I ever fallen in love so quickly. There isn't a part of my being that's protesting this..."

I couldn't make my mouth express what my heart was experiencing. The charge between us, I knew wasn't meant to last for a weekend. The more I was in his presence the charge intensified.

"Shit," he blew breaking our stare. "You don't..."

"No," I found one word, but the rest were caught in my throat. His eyes grew sad while I forced the words from the depths. "I do... I am... I mean – Antonio, I love you."

I watched his chest move while his brain sent the signal to his lungs that it was ok to breathe again. That smile crossed his face as he hooked my chin gently with his hand. "I know you've been hurt and you're going to want to run away. When you want to run from me just hold on tighter, okay?"

"Okay," nodding my head I let the smile I tried to suppress take over my lips.

Finally, dressed and ready to close out Ashley's birthday weekend I headed down the stairs to see Ashley, Keisha, and Alisha standing at the bottom of the stairs with their arms folded.

"All that shit Anton gives me about not being fast, and he can't even let you out the room," Ashley kissed her teeth.

"Girl," he blew from the room. "We're grown."

"Mmhmm," Ashley rolled her eyes. "Ms. James are you ready to go?"

"We should leave now before your brother gets his hands on me again," laughing I grabbed my purse and headed out to my car.

"I swear, he's a mess," she blew climbing into the back seat with Keisha.

Shaking my head, I climbed in the driver's seat and started the engine. "I don't know what kind of diamonds you got buried deep within, Kaliah, but my brother is wide open. He's never been like this with anyone. Not even that gold-digging ex."

"No?" Alisha asked with a smirk as I pulled out the driveway.

"Nope. In fact, she was the devil. She was the type to smile in your face and the minute you were out of sight start talking reckless. My poor brother is so nice that he wasn't going to be the guy to put her out. Instead, he behaved himself in Philly until she left him. That's just how he is. Some people will say he's stupid or soft, but his regard for women is high," I heard her voice smile a little. "He's just different. Please, don't hurt him. He's so good, there are not many men like him left."

I loved the way Ashley thought so highly of Antonio, it only solidified that what I was feeling was okay to feel. After Daniel, I wasn't sure if I would love, love again. I knew that I wanted it, but I didn't want to put my heart through the trouble of getting on the treadmill to nowhere to find it.

Finding her eyes in the rear-view mirror, I smiled. Smiling back at me, I made her a silent promise. Turning her gaze to the sight of the hills, she still wore a satisfied smiled on her face.

Ashley and Keisha were like kids in the candy store on Rodeo. We were in the fourth store, and the girls were enjoying themselves and the credit card that they coaxed from Antonio.

"So," Alisha started looking in the mirror at a pair of sunglasses she was trying on.

"So," I replied predicting where this conversation was going to go.

"Is it love or is it excellent sex and you can't tell the difference?" she questioned looking at me for approval on the gawky glasses on her face. "Yes or no?"

"No," I frowned. "You know, I said I wasn't going to do this."

"Mmhmm, I heard that when you were crying over that divorce instead of celebrating. Remember what I said?" placing the current pair on the counter before trying on another.

"That love would hit me out of nowhere," I recited her encouraging words with an eye roll.

"Was I right or was I right?"

"You were right, but you seem too skeptical."

"I'm going to be skeptical of anyone who enters your life because you are giving, and you don't know any other way to be. Hell, if your daddy popped up, I'd be giving him the side eye too," she scoffed. The statement caused my lip to curl.

"I doubt I'm on his radar. At this point what can he do for me? I'll be thirty in seven months, what is he going to teach me?" I questioned, looking at her give up trying to find sunglasses that didn't make her look like a bug.

"Forgiveness," answering with simplicity she shrugged her shoulders. "You know how to do everything but forgive someone."

I detested the fact she could read me like a book. "Hmm."

"Hmm," she mocked.

"What else is on your mind, you've been off since the party last night," just as well as she knew me, I knew her.

"Peter wants to start a family…"

"That's great so why the pause?"

"Because it means that I'll be leaving you on your own. The idea of being superwoman is grand, but I have to realistic with myself." Her voice was sad, and the news definitely tugged at my heartstrings.

"Lisha," I sighed. "You won't be leaving me alone. I want you to be happy. I want you and Peter to enjoy your life together. Yeah, I'll miss you, but I won't be far. Plus, I'd love our relationship to be strictly personal."

"I bet you would," she laughed. "You know I love you?"

"I've never doubted that. Can we stop this? You know I don't like to cry," huffing and fanning my eyes, I stepped back.

"I know, I'm sorry," she laughed. "We also want you to be the godmother when the time comes."

"Oh my God, stop!" I pleaded with my eyes swelling. "I would love that!"

We enjoyed the rest of our time together until we had to return to the house. Antonio, Ashley, and Keisha were set to fly back to South Carolina tonight, and I dreaded the idea. I did everything in my power to prolong this day. Shopping, lunch, manicures and pedicures, and a ride around the Hills. But we had to return home.

Dragging myself and my bags into the house after seeing Alisha off, I carried my bags upstairs.

"Ashley," Antonio started up the minute the door closed. "Really?"

Laughing lowly, I shook my head. All he saw were the bags, I wasn't going to tell him that half of it was my treat. "Did you buy everything?"

"Oh, relax," she blew shooing him off.

"You see how she treats me?" he asked walking into my bedroom.

"She loves you. She's your little sister, she's supposed to give you a hard time," I laughed, putting my bags in the closet.

"What do you have planned for the next couple of days?" he asked as he walked into the closet and leaned on the dresser in the middle of the room.

"Read over these new scripts," I shared. "And pout that you're not going to be here."

"You don't have to pout, and you can read the scripts on the plane," he stated causing me to pin my brows together.

"What are you talking about?"

"I might've broken down and mentioned you to my mother, who may have invited you to come to the great state of South Carolina for a few days."

"Antonio."

"Kaliah."

There was no need to protest this. I'd already climbed on the diving board and jumped into thirteen feet of water without any floatation devices. What harm could Antonio's parents actually do?

"What's the weather like?" seeing his face light up, I returned the smile.

"Cold," smiling that million-dollar smile, he unknowingly settled my nerves. "Don't be nervous, they're cool."

"Mm, I'm not worried about them," I frowned pulling out a suitcase.

"They'll love you. Trust me."

ANTONIO CLARK

*M*y mom didn't even let Kaliah fully into the house before she had her arms wrapped around her, hugging the life out of her. "I mean, I'm not important at all," I chuckled holding my bags, Ashley's, and Kaliah's.

"First of all, everything isn't about you," Ashley interjected causing me to curl my lip and flip her the bird.

"You are beautiful," my mother stepped back examining Kaliah. "You know since Anton's been away, he's never bought anyone home."

"You're kidding," Kaliah chuckled nervously. "What about…"

"Jada?" my father blew before kissing his teeth. "We happened to meet her at a football game. He knew better than to bring that in this house."

Watching as Kaliah's eyes popped out her head and her cover her mouth with her hand, I shook my head. "Alright, that's enough. We're leaving."

"Would you stop being so sensitive?" my mother asked leading Kaliah into the house. "I don't know what you did to my son, but please keep it up."

"I'll try," Kaliah laughed nervously.

"I hope you aren't on one of those Hollywood diets. We are having barbecue for dinner," my father spoke up.

"Oh dad, she isn't one of those avocado toast L.A. girls," Ashley informed. "She's a perfect fit for us."

"I can tell," my mother beamed before landing her eyes on me. "You want to show her to the guest room and get her settled?"

"Yes ma'am," I nodded climbing the stairs behind Kaliah.

"Your parents are so nice," she smiled. "Your mom reminds me a lot of mine."

"She's always been the neighborhood mom. Even still, everyone gets Sunday dinner, and everyone is invited over for Thanksgiving dinner," I shared walking past Eddie's room to see the door open, and cleared out. Coming to a standstill, I stood at the entrance and looked in.

The posters were gone, clothes and shoes were gone, too. We all thought that she would've done this after Eddie passed, but mom wanted to hold on to his memory for as long as she could. I never processed how I would feel standing here looking into an empty room that was once full of his things. The only thing that was in here was her sewing table and a tall lamp in the corner.

"Are you okay?" Kaliah's hand on my back brought me back to the present.

"Yeah," I was proud of mom for finally taking this step to closure. "This used to be Eddie's room. She finally did something with it. She finally let him go."

Kaliah smiled. It wasn't her usual smile, it was a smile of peace. We understood what it was like to lose someone close to us, she also understood what it meant to let them go.

"Come on," pulling myself away from the room I continued down the hall to the guest room. Putting her bags in the closet, I watched as the smile on her face didn't fade. It grew wider and her eyes flooded with tears.

"I feel like I'm at home. I haven't felt like this in years," she announced, wiping her face. "You don't understand how much this means to me."

Enveloping her in my arms and pressing my forehead against hers, I kissed her face. "I want to give you whatever you're lacking."

"I swear, you are perfect," she laughed wiping her face.

"Not perfect."

"You're right, you snore, and you talk in your sleep while hogging the covers."

"Y'all come on, dinner is going to be cold!" Ashley shouted up the stairs. "You got to keep your eye on them, they're sickening."

"That damn girl," groaning and stepping away from her, I took her hand in mine. "You good?"

"I'm good."

Joining the rest of the family around the dining room table, my mother took it upon herself to fix Kaliah's plate. "Good grief woman, where is she going to put all that food?"

"Don't you worry Mr. Clark," Kaliah shared with a soft laugh. "My trainer might kill me when I get back, but there's going to be nothing left on this plate when I'm finished."

"Oh, really?" pops smirked across the table at me. "Alright, son. You did well."

"I think I did, too."

"Mom, I have to tell you about my trip!" Ashley took over the rest of the conversation which I was grateful for. The feelings Kaliah and I had for each other had already been established. She was overwhelmed being here and I didn't want her to shut down with a million and one questions.

After dinner, Ashley, Kaliah, and mom disappeared into the kitchen to clean up leaving pops and me alone. Sitting in the living room with pops, he looked over at me. "How are you feeling?"

He usually asked this question when I was at a pivotal

point in my life. I'd only heard it twice before. "Whole."

Nodding his head, he smirked lightly. "I can tell. She's nice, your mother likes her. Your sister loves her, and so do you."

"I swore when you were going on about you know when you've met your wife within three minutes of laying eyes on her that you were smoking something," I laughed.

"Bit you in the ass didn't it?" his hearty laugh filled the room. "Got you walking around with your nose open."

"Pops, this is crazy."

"It is. Your mother and I have been together for forty-five years. I remember walking over to her and her friends and telling her she was going to be my wife. Of course, she laughed at me and blew it off, but a year later we were married. We haven't looked back." Their love had always been one to mirror.

They drilled what love looked like into our heads. They were so in tune with one another that they knew when something wasn't right with other. Pops could look at mom and say what she was thinking, she hated when he did that. She would fuss and tell him to let her get her own thoughts out.

"How'd you do it?" I asked. I wasn't ready to run down the aisle yet, but I knew Kaliah and I would eventually end up there.

"Never stop learning. Kaliah is going to change over and over again. She'll evolve into a better woman time after time and when she does you have to evolve into a better man for her. Never stop dating, never stop appreciating her. When a woman is loved correctly, they become a magnificent well of love, and it doesn't run dry. I've raised you to protect and to provide, it goes beyond just financial stability. That's important too, but you have to provide her with security. No other woman can compare to the one that has your back and your front. You have to protect her emotions, her mind, her spirit, and her being. You do that, and she'll love you more than you

91

could love yourself. That's the key to keeping a last happy marriage. Hell, any relationship," he shared. Pops liked to call himself the love doctor. "Love comes differently to everyone. It's like a race, you know. You can't just run the race and win without training. We have to go through the training. The bad relationships, the aftermath of rebuilding who we are, and after a while, we have the stamina to run the race and win. I'm not telling you every day is going to be great. It won't be, but if you love each other, you trust each other, and you respect each other you can't lose."

"Real shit," I recited Eddie's favorite line.

"Real shit."

Kaliah James

MY HEART WAS SO FULL. NOT ONLY HAD ANTONIO CAME INTO MY life like a whirlwind and showed me that my idea of love was off, but he also didn't let up. At times, his love could be overwhelming, and I felt undeserving of it. He quickly reminded me that I deserved more, and he just hadn't figured out how to give it to me yet. There were days where my brain would try to talk me out of this to protect my heart. Even with that slither of doubt I knew that this was that earth-shattering, soul snatching love that my mother used to talk about. She would say, "I want you to have everything I didn't. A full life with someone who loves you enough to force you to share your world." I knew she would be happy to see me now.

I'd been back in L.A. for three months, and Antonio had been back and forth. The minute I really started to miss him, he'd show up. "You think you know someone and you find out they can't cook," he joked throwing some garlic into the pan.

"You never asked. Who are you making all of this food for?" I questioned. "I know I can eat but who else is coming over here?"

"You'll see soon. Right now, you're being a bad sous chef," he pointed to the onion lying on the counter that I had yet to chop up for him. "You either cry now or cry later."

"I'll take later for two hundred, Alex," he shook his head and snickered.

"What am I going to do about you?"

"Your only option is to love me," I teased placing my wine glass down and grabbing a knife to cut the onion with.

A half an hour had passed before the doorbell rang. "I got it," Antonio announced leaving me at the dining room table alone. It was set up to see if I was going to start eating without him. I was almost sure of it.

Returning to the dining room with a tall, dark skin man, I looked over at the two oddly. "What's going on?"

"Kaliah," the man's voice broke while he examined me. "Baby girl."

Hitting me like a ton of bricks I squeezed my eyes shut trying to wake myself up. "I'm so sorry."

I wasn't expecting this to be my reaction of laying eyes on my father for the first time to be like this. I wanted to be angry with him. I wanted to hate him for leaving me. Seeing his face and hearing his voice, my heart wouldn't let me. Letting the tears flow freely from my eyes, I shook my head in disbelief.

His presence was so heavy, I couldn't stop crying. Bent over in the seat, I sobbed into the palm of my hands. His arms wrapped around me and his nose nuzzled into my curls. The violent cry was agonizing.

"Where have you been?" I sobbed into his chest. "Why did you leave me? How come you could love the rest of them and not love me? What did I do?"

As a grown woman I had so many questions for the little

girl in me that just wanted her daddy. I needed them answered.

"I'm so sorry," he cried. "I didn't want to leave you."

"Then why did you leave us?" I asked muffled with my face pressing against his chest.

"I got into some trouble. I had to go. There wasn't a day I didn't think about you. I watched every movie you've been in, every show, and every interview you did," he shared. "I wanted so badly to reach out to you."

"Why didn't you? You let me go through life for twenty-nine years without you! Who does that to their child?" I asked breaking away from him. "You ran away and left me. I had to figure this shit out alone. Mom could only teach me so much. I needed you, and you weren't there. You weren't there to protect me. Do you know how that feels!? The thought of you loving all your other kids while I was the one that got left behind killed me. It still hurts like hell. Every day I fight not to blame myself for you leaving. You ran and you never looked back. Momma struggled to make sure I had half of what everyone else had when she couldn't afford to give me nothing! She died still trying to play your role."

Pulling myself away from him I stood to my feet. "I don't care that you were in trouble. I hated you from the moment I realized that you were never going to come back."

"Kaliah," Antonio started.

"Where did you find him?" I asked not taking my eyes off the shameful expression that consumed my father's face.

"I flew him in from Kentucky," Antonio shared.

"Send him back," walking away from the both of them I could hear his sigh of defeat.

"Don't leave, I'll go talk to her," Antonio directed following me outside.

"You should've run this by me before you bombarded me like that," I spoke up feeling him behind me. "He didn't even try. Do you know how that makes me feel? I'll tell you. It makes me feel like I wasn't good enough. Like he regretted even having me. How dare he? How dare he?"

Pulling my reluctant being into his chest, he didn't say anything else he just rubbed my back and let me cry until I was settled enough. "You can't run from this. You have questions and you need the answers. If you aren't satisfied with them, you can let him go. But baby, please don't let him walk out of here without at least knowing. You have every right to be mad as hell but he owes you an explanation, and it's up to you to require at least that."

"Okay," I finally spoke up after a moment of chewing on the inside of my cheek. Following Antonio back into the house, I took my seat and looked across the table at my father. I noticed I looked so much like him after years of thinking that I got my features from my mother. "I'm waiting, and you got to come better than you were in trouble. It's been damn near thirty years."

"Where would you like me to start?" he asked.

"Anywhere is better than nowhere."

"Your mother and I moved from Virginia to Alabama because I had a job offer down there. It was a good one, too. A few days after your mother telling me that we were expecting you I went out with some friends from work to celebrate the news. We were a group of young black men working in Alabama. It might've been the late eighties, but that didn't stop white men from reminding us that there some places we didn't belong. One thing led to another, words were exchanged, fists were thrown, and I took a bottle and knocked one of the guys across the head. He fell so hard that he died from the impact. The only thing I could think about was running. I had enough money for a train ticket, and I got the hell out of there. I was so scared, Kaliah. I didn't want to leave you or your mom but what good was I going to be to you in prison," he explained.

"Let me get this right, to avoid prison for yourself you put me in it without remorse. Call me selfish, but you killed a man and ran away because you were scared. So, you've been so scared for twenty-nine years that you couldn't send so much as a bat signal? Wow."

"If I could take back what I did to you and your mother, I would but I can't," he hung his head. "All I have is right now. I don't know how Antonio found me because I changed my name, but I'm here. I don't get to come into your life and pretend to be a father to the little girl. If you let me, we can start here and build a relationship."

"How do I know you won't leave me again?"

"You have my word. I see the damage my absence did to you. I don't ever want to impose that pain on you again," he shared. Every fiber of my being wanted to believe him.

"You get one shot with me. One," I made it very clear. No one was going to come into my life anymore to raise hell and leave. All he had was this one opportunity to prove to me that he deserved to be here.

Continuing with dinner, I talked to him until I was fighting to stay awake. "Baby girl, I'm going to get going. Antonio told me to be over in the morning for breakfast."

"Are you going to be here?"

"I will," he assured. "I am very proud of you."

Brushing his thumb across my cheek like mom used to do, he smiled warmly before leaving. Watching the driver disappear down the road, I closed the door and headed upstairs to find Antonio laying in the bed watching ESPN.

"On a scale of one to ten, how mad are you at me?" he asked as I climbed in the bed and laid my head on his chest.

"I'm not mad anymore, I know why you did it. I appreciate you because you didn't have to make sure I got what I needed."

"I told you, I wanted to give everything you lacked. You need your dad, baby."

"I never believed that until tonight."

EPILOGUE

2 years later
Valentine's Day

Kaliah James

*E*verything was swollen, my face, my feet, and my hands. I could barely breathe let alone move, and my irritation was high. Everywhere I went around this house Antonio followed me with a camera. He said it was so he wouldn't miss any of the final moments of this pregnancy. With him being gone most of the season these last few days were critical for him.

"Baby, please," I begged. "Can I have just a few hours without you and that damn camera?"

"Then I'll miss something," he shook his head rejecting my plea. "This is our last Valentine's day before we become parents. Anything you want to tell our baby girl?"

"Your daddy is annoying, and you're kicking my bladder," I groaned running my fat fingers over my belly. My hands were so fat my wedding ring had to be worn around my neck. "But I can't wait to meet you and get my body back. When I do, your daddy is never touching me again."

"You talk a good game baby but you and I both know that's not going to happen," Antonio chuckled before placing the camera down on the coffee table.

We were now living in Georgia. We were close to his family and my dad. My dad and I were making strides in our relationship, and I was building a relationship with my siblings. I was at a point in life where I had everything I wanted. A husband that smothered me with love even when I got on his nerves in the worst way. A father who was making it a point to be present in my life after so much lost time. Even Alisha and Peter were close to us. Once Antonio and I exchanged 'I do's' last year, and he announced he was going to play his final season in Atlanta, Alisha and Peter didn't think twice about moving. It worked out as Peter was looking to expand his business and Alisha didn't want to be too far away from me. I didn't want to be too far from her or my goddaughter Ariel either. Over the last two years, Peter and Antonio had also become great friends.

"Are you excited?" I asked staring at my huge belly sitting in my lap. "You're retiring from football, we have a whole human arriving at any moment, and I'm taking a break from acting. You sure you're going to be used to being in my space all the time?"

"Where am I going to go?" he questioned with a hearty laugh. "I don't have any options. I'll be right here in your space with our daughter thinking about how much life we have ahead of us. There is nowhere I'd rather be than right here. I was born ready. I told you I can do anything."

"I hear you talking," I replied moving the pillows behind me to get more comfortable.

"I got you, didn't I?" he asked grinning from ear to ear. "Not only did I get you in the mountains, but I also got you to say I do and to have my baby. You haven't learned yet?"

"I was actually hoping to keep forgetting so you can keep reminding me," his smile still did it for me. I didn't want anyone else but him. He knew what I was thinking and before I could open my mouth to say it, he would. It drove me crazy.

What really blew my mind was how fast his love had come in and thrown my inhibitions to the wind. He consumed me with such a radical feeling of love that I never wanted to feel anything else but his love for me. Even on our bad days, his love was always at the forefront. He would say, "Woman you are on my last damn nerve, but I love you. I love you more than you could know." At times I thought it was reverse psychology to make me calm down on my crazy.

"I will remind you until I'm dead and gone, but even then, I think I could find some way to remind you that you'll always be the reason my heart beats. The reason I don't give up when it's so easy to. You'll always be mine. My sweet sweet Valentine. Say you'll always be."

"You're so corny," I snorted with laughter.

"Say it," he coaxed.

"I'll be your Valentine."

"I will always be your Valentine," placing a hand on my belly his kissed my lips and then my belly. "I love you too."

"We love you, baby. Thank you."

"I'm at your service always."

Love rushed in like light searching for darkness, illuminating every depth I closed off. I was fully submerged in its warmth. I never wanted to feel its bitter aftertaste again. I was going to delight in this sweet taste of unequivocal love for as long as God saw fit.

The End.

UNTITLED

Thank you for reading.
Join Aubreé Pynn's Pynn Pals to share your thoughts on this book.
For exclusive sneak peeks like my author page: AubreéPynn
Connect with me on my personal Facebook page:
Aubreé Pynn
To purchase signed paperbacks visit
www.apxcb.com

Made in the USA
Middletown, DE
18 January 2026

27224993R00060